Tales From
Valleyview Cemetery

John Brhel & J. Sullivan

CEMETERY GATES
MEDIA

Tales From Valleyview Cemetery
Published by Cemetery Gates Media
Binghamton, NY

ISBN: 978-1537024929

Printed in the USA by CreateSpace

For more information about this book and other Cemetery Gates Media publications, visit us at:

cemeterygatesmedia.tumblr.com
facebook.com/cemeterygatesmedia
twitter.com/cemeterygatesm

Cover illustration and design by Chad Wehrle
Interior illustration "Charlie" by Chad Wehrle

CONTENTS

INTRODUCTION

Welcome to Valleyview, where bodies lie buried but an ancient curse never sleeps...

The stories in this book are meant to stand individually, as legends, chillers, and tales of terror for a reader to consume at his or her leisure. However, there are additional themes and narratives that travel from story to story, rarely sequentially, that an astute reader may patch together to obtain a bigger picture of what it means to live, work, and play in the presence of Valleyview Cemetery and its centuries-old curse.

Valleyview is the heart and soul of Lestershire, while the curse itself predates the town and the cemetery's formation. Each story is meant to add additional character to the land and the people it serves—sometimes dark and malicious, sometimes playful and altruistic.

There are appendices referred to at the end of three of the stories. They can be read at the end of each tale for additional insight, or saved for future curiosity about recurring characters and motifs.

The notes section is meant to serve as an accompaniment to the appendices, in assisting a reader who might be interested in more information about each story, from an authorial perspective.

There is more than meets the eye in ol' Valleyview. Dig deep enough and you'll find horrors both unimaginable and oddly familiar. When you piece it all together, you'll see that this cemetery is one unique resting place.

Enjoy your visit (just make sure to leave before dark.)

John and Joe
October 2015

Angel Music

On her walk to work one morning, Brenda Wells heard the faint sound of a pipe organ as she passed the local cemetery. She thought nothing of the music, and continued down Memorial Drive to her small office space which overlooked the river. The cemetery, like so many other local landmarks, held little to no memory for her—as she had only come to Lestershire as an adult to attend college.

It was a warm spring morning the next time she passed the cemetery and heard the organ music. She had left her apartment early, so she had a moment to pause and listen. She thought back to her Romantic Period music class in freshman year, which was probably the last time she had really *listened* to Classical-era compositions.

The music could have been Brahms, she thought. *Schicksalslied* was her all-time favorite orchestra piece, and she remembered some of his organ chorales distinctly, as they were tested for on the final exam. She recalled listening to some of those works dozens of times during the last week of class. As she walked, she paid close attention to the execution; even to a layperson it would be obvious the performer was exemplary.

When she passed the main gate she saw two girls playing tag just off the entrance roadway, among a few of the taller obelisks. Brenda passed under the gate, curious about the children, who looked about eight or nine years old.

"Hi, girls. Isn't there school today?" She smiled at the pair as she startled them from their game. The girls turned to face her. When she saw their eyes she instinctively shuddered. Both sets were obviously cataract, a filmy white fog obscured their irises.

"We don't go to the public school. The kids make fun of us," said the smaller of the two. Brenda felt sorry for the girls and remembered how terrible children could be to one another.

"I'm sorry to hear that," said Brenda as the girls came over to her. "Where's the music coming from?"

The girls pointed toward a stone chapel that was blocked from street view by a row of bushes and pines. Strangely, the organ seemed fainter from inside the cemetery. Brenda looked at her watch and knew she had to be on her way, so she thanked the girls and left.

The next morning as Brenda passed the cemetery, the organ was inarguably louder than the day before. She had listened to a few of her older CDs from school the previous night and was sure the organist was playing a Brahm's piece. The girls were jumping rope just inside the cemetery gate and she went in to talk with them again.

"How's it going, ladies?"

The girls stopped jumping and greeted her warmly.

"Hello, ma'am," said the shorter girl, her milky-white eyes looking dead in the sunlight.

Brenda was concerned the girls might be neglected, so she asked them again about their schooling. "Do you go to the Catholic elementary down the road?"

The girls paused. The delayed manner in which they reacted to her voice made Brenda think that they might both be blind.

"We don't go to school," said the taller child. Brenda figured they were homeschooled.

"Then who's watching over you?" She looked around. The cemetery was empty as far as she could tell; no one was visiting or cutting the grass.

"Our angel," the girls replied in near unison. Brenda was confused by what they meant. She thought about the organ that had been continually playing while she visited with them.

"Who—the organ player?"

They nodded.

Brenda continued, "Will they be mad if I pop in and listen?" It was already 8:45. She was too curious about the situation, the girls, and the music at that point to worry about being late for work.

"Angel loves visitors," said the smaller child.

Brenda smiled at the girls and walked the path to the chapel.

As she approached the stone structure and its big wooden doors, the music seemed to increase in volume and intensity. Brenda's pulse quickened in time with the tune. Her body was consumed by the power of the organ as she nudged one of the heavy doors open.

She walked the main aisle, studying the dark interior of the chapel, which seemed much bigger than it had appeared from the outside. The ornate, stained-glass windows were its only light source, shining mostly on the center interior. The pews were older—a rich, dark wood—and the carpet was well-worn. She could just make out a figure seated at the organ off to the left side of the raised altar area.

As the figure continued to play, her heart raced. A sense of foreboding arose within her, but she advanced to the front of the chapel, driven by curiosity. The figure didn't seem to notice or care that she had entered, and she couldn't speak up and let him know she was there due to the overwhelming power of the music.

Brenda approached the seated figure, who seemed to be enshrouded within a black robe. When she was a few paces away the music stopped—though the organist didn't immediately reveal himself.

"Sorry to disturb you, your playing is beautiful and…" She froze when the hooded figure stood, turning to face her. What she saw could only be described as demonic; a leathery, burnt face with red-lit eyes.

"Oh, my God!" Her shriek was cut short as a long, crooked knife appeared from beneath the robe and drove into her soft center. She gasped and choked on blood; a rivulet crawled down her lip and cheek as she fell to the floor of the chapel, motionless.

Brenda slowly faded from the world of the living on that chapel floor, but before she left consciousness she saw the two girls in the frame of the open door. She watched the hooded figure walk toward them and had enough wits about her to rasp a barely audible warning.

The demon reached in its robe as if to draw the knife— but instead revealed a puppy, handing it to one of the girls.

"Thank you, Angel!" The girls were overjoyed at their new toy and returned to the cemetery to play. The door closed behind them and Brenda's last vision of life was that of the approaching horror.

Married, Buried

"I'll be back in twenty minutes, dear," said Peter Reynolds to his wife, Maggie, as he put on his coat and stepped out of his beige ranch home for his evening walk. He walked down Memorial Drive, past the model homes of his neighbors, and stopped in front of Murphy's Delicatessen, a big grin on his face.

"Good evening, Shirley," he said as he approached the thin brunette standing outside.

"Hi, Peter," said Shirley. She was tall and graceful, with a flattering waistline and an ass to match. She was dressed in a smart, white blouse and a pair of tight-fitting Gloria Vanderbilt jeans with a little swan on the back pocket.

The pair walked the neighborhood together, mocking their spouses, discussing the previous night's episode of *All in the Family*, laughing, flirting.

From the kitchen window of that beige ranch up the hill, Maggie Reynolds watched her husband as she scrubbed dried-up potatoes off his dinner plate. *That's the third night this week I've seen him with that shrew!* thought Maggie. *It can't be a coincidence. I'm no fool.*

A few houses down, looking out the front window of his baby-blue ranch, was Shirley's husband, Ted. *What's that son of a bitch think he's doing?* he thought as he cleaned the barrel of his pistol with a soft, yellow cloth.

Later that night, Peter and Shirley caught hell from their spouses. Accusations were made. Fingers pointed. Someone's face may have been slapped.

"Why are you always walking with that guy?"

"Are you and Shirley Elliott best buddies now? Hmmm?"

"I don't want to see you with that asshole again, you got it?"

"What's *she* got that *I* don't have?"

The jig was up. It was obvious to anybody with a pulse that Peter and Shirley weren't meeting up every night by accident—and Shirley had a black eye to prove it.

The secret lovers decided that they would have to meet in a more secluded place from that point on. Valleyview Cemetery seemed like an odd choice, at first. Mausoleums and the constant specter of Death aren't necessarily the keys to a romantic evening, but it was private.

A few nights later, Shirley was standing next to a grave with the name Wintermute carved into it when Peter came walking down the cemetery path.

"I was worried you wouldn't show," said Peter, grinning. "Thought you'd be too creeped out."

Shirley laughed. "Hey, I'll put up with ghosts and zombies if it keeps me away from Ted for an hour." Peter held out his hand and Shirley took hold of it, firmly, absolutely.

They walked for a while before kissing against a mausoleum like foolhardy teenagers. Ted grabbed Shirley and pulled her in close. As they made out, they crossed a barrier they hadn't dared cross before. They explored new avenues of their relationship as they moved from grave to grave, tumbling and caressing on hallowed ground.

To say that Maggie gave Peter "shit" for coming home two hours after leaving for a leisurely evening walk would be a massive understatement. She berated him, called him a good-for-nothing. Said he would never measure up as a father. She might as well have cut off his balls and mailed them to Siberia.

Peter spent the night in his car. The next morning, he woke up with a sore neck and the stark realization that things couldn't go on this way. He was in too deep with Maggie—they had co-signed a loan for their house just nine months prior. It had to stop.

A couple days later, after things had cooled down, Peter walked into Valleyview to break it off with Shirley. Though only nights had passed since they'd last seen each other, the cemetery seemed as if it had grown darker, the graves crowded closer together. He didn't recall feeling this uneasy the first time they had met there, but now the place gave him the creeps.

Shirley stood at Mr. Wintermute's grave, a broken look on her face. She gave Peter a little half-smile as he approached.

"Hi, Peter."

"Hi, Shirley." Peter bit his lip and shuffled his feet on the gravel pathway. "We need to talk."

Shirley's eyes opened wide and the moon reflected off her pupils, making them look like shimmering pools. "Peter. I know this seems crazy, but I think we could make this work. If we just—"

"Don't." He cut her off before she could change his mind (*and with eyes like those, it wouldn't take much*, he thought.) "This can't go on any longer. They know, alright? We knew this would never work..."

There was the sound of footsteps rapidly approaching and Peter felt someone suddenly grab him by the neck. Before he had time to react or see who had attacked him, he was thrown to the ground, next to a cold, hard tombstone. A few inches closer and he would have had an instant lobotomy.

He looked up to see his neighbor, Ted Elliott, standing over him with a frenzied look in his eyes. Ted was an ass, but the worst Peter had ever seen him was the day he had run over a tree stump and broke his new lawnmower. He thought Ted was angry *that* day.

Ted picked him up by the shirt collar and was about to throw him back down again, but Peter swept his leg and the two of them fell to the ground. They rolled around, trading punches, socks to the head and gut. Peter found himself on top of Ted and brought down both of his fists on his chest like he was a choking victim. Ted let out a harsh wheeze as Peter's balled-up fists connected with his body.

Peter was about to bring his fists down for another round when a large rock struck his skull, unleashing a flurry of blood and sending him thumping to the ground. Ted looked over to see his wife, Shirley, holding the blood-soaked rock in her trembling hands. She dropped to her knees and started wailing.

"What have I done!?" she screamed, her cries echoing throughout the cemetery. Ted walked over to her and stared, mouth agape. "I had to do it, Ted! He was going to kill you."

She was delirious. "I know; I know it was wrong of me. It was just a fling; you hear? He didn't mean anything. It was just a fling. This little voice in my head said I had to help you, Ted. Then it was just screaming at me—I can't explain it. And when I saw him coming down on you like that. Oh, I just couldn't take it. I love you, Ted!"

Ted pressed the palm of his hand firmly over her mouth. "Shut up! Just shut up, right now! Do you realize what you've done?" He looked down at Peter, who lay on the ground, motionless. "You *killed* the good-for-nothing bastard."

Without saying another word, he walked away. Shirley sat on the grass, her eyes frozen, staring at the body of her lover.

Ted returned a minute later, holding a shovel he lifted from the caretaker's shed. He walked to an overgrown, seemingly neglected corner of the cemetery and started digging. When he was done he walked back toward where Shirley knelt in the grass crying silently, his clothes covered in dirt and blood—his and Peter's.

"Help me carry him," said Ted. He looked at her as if he would snap her neck if she didn't comply. They each picked up

14

one side of Peter's body—Ted, the legs; Shirley, the head, though she strained to hold her end—and carried him over to the freshly dug hole.

They dropped his body into the shallow grave and Ted picked the shovel back up like he was doing any other routine job in the back garden. He started to dump the dirt over Peter when Shirley jumped in and started weeping on Peter's chest.

"Don't!" yelled Shirley. "Ted, what are we doing? This is *Peter Reynolds*! You used to be in the same bowling league. He helped us clean up when the basement flooded last spring. I know what I did was wrong, something hideous just took ahold of me. I'll make it up to you and the Lord—but please, we can't do this! We have to turn ourselves in. I mean, is he even *dead*? How do we know for sure?" She put her head to Peter's chest.

Ted held the shovel in his hands, gripping the handle tighter and tighter. The more Shirley cried, and the more he thought of her screwing Peter, the more he wanted to act.

Suddenly, he felt the shovel torn from his hands and he turned to see Maggie Reynolds holding it. He hadn't ever seen her hold anything heavier than a trayful of finger foods. Shirley stood, facing her husband and former lover's wife, resigned to their final judgment.

"Oh, shut your trap you cheating whore," said Maggie as she whacked Shirley in the face with the shovel. Blood gushed from her open wound and she fell over, landing on top of her former lover. Shirley lay in the shallow grave, seemingly as motionless as Peter.

Ted looked at Maggie. Without saying a word, she handed the shovel back to him and he threw dirt over the unmarked burial of Peter Reynolds and Shirley Elliott. Ted and Maggie had both noticed a slight shifting in the dirt as it accumulated, but neither spoke of it that night or any time after.

It wasn't long before the whole neighborhood found out. Peter and Shirley had been having an affair and they'd run off together.

Ted Elliott and Maggie Reynolds were often seen walking the neighborhood. Most folks assumed they were just helping each other cope with the betrayal of their spouses. They always avoided Valleyview Cemetery, though. And who could blame them? What would make good people want to walk through a foul place like that?

Other Voices, Other Tombs

The backyard of Jeff's parents' house met the pointed iron fence of the cemetery. In childhood, he experienced an unnamed dread as he looked out of his bedroom window at the jagged stone rows and the new graves as they opened and closed. He always had a general uneasiness that he never really expressed to his family about his daily view. Eventually, he became an adult and the cemetery faded into his subconscious. His youthful trepidation buried by all of his worldly worries and grown-up responsibilities.

His parents were dead ten years when he moved his daughter home. He thought it odd how he lay in his parents' old room and still thought of it as *their* house. He made a nursery for his daughter, Georgia, in his childhood bedroom. It was just the two of them, all alone on Richard Street.

August was warmer than usual and Jeff had no air conditioning. He was constantly worried about Georgia overheating at night. He kept her window open for most of the summer, and they would often sit in the rocker after he got home from work and stare out at the graveyard. There was a particular group of stone angels he liked to meditate on during those long afternoons and evenings.

The traffic during the day was constant. All weekend and most nights he would listen to the Little League baseball announcers in the nearby park as they read the young boys' names, many the sons of long-lost school chums. But after ten, closer to midnight, it was dead silent and completely relaxing—though often lonely with just the baby for company. His friends all had families and they were often out of touch.

Late one night, when Georgia was sound asleep and he was starting to drift off in his own bed, he began hearing parts of conversations over the baby monitor.

TALES FROM VALLEYVIEW CEMETERY

"Speak to the Russian."

"*Bin gar keine Russin, stamm' aus Litauen, echt deut-sch.*"

"Slavs, the lot of you. Frick is rolling a big cigar, laughing."

It seemed like multiple male voices, each one distinct. It was obviously not coming from Georgia's room. He had messed with walkie-talkies, various electronic handhelds since he was a kid, and remembered picking up what seemed like phone conversations from time to time. They would come in clear for a few seconds then fade.

"When the grave has been made, we will make it still better." This was strange because the feed was not fizzling and the speech seemed to be getting louder.

"We will adorn it, and cover it with moss."

"We will do this, we three brothers." The way the final line was said in unison made Jeff shiver. He heard nothing more that night.

Early the next morning Jeff's brother, Arnold, stopped by with his daughter to visit.

"She's getting big, Jeff." Arnold sat in the rocker in the nursery with his four year-old in his lap. He had a huge house up on the hill, a gorgeous wife and he owned a successful surveying company.

"It's tough, man," said Jeff. Arnold nodded and stared out at the cemetery.

"Hey, I heard some bizarre conversation over the baby monitor last night." His brother smirked. Jeff continued, "It sounded like a bunch of the old guys down at Charlie's Pub shit-talking, but they were going on about making graves. It was pretty creepy."

Arnold laughed. "Remember when we played hide and seek out there." He pointed at the group of mausoleums farther up the cemetery hill. Jeff nodded, recalling when he fell and broke his leg and all the trouble they got in.

18

"Once in a while I'll see kids sitting up on that one," said Jeff.

Arnold chuckled. "They're still doing that?" Jeff nodded.

In high school, he, Arnold and their buddies were messing around in the cemetery, late at night. Jeff broke his leg when he fell from the roof of one of the older mausoleums.

"I swear someone pushed me." They both laughed. Word spread that Jeff was attacked by a ghost. So, for years teenagers came down and sat on that same mausoleum to see if they could meet the supernatural themselves.

"Anyway, I heard a name in that conversation last night: Frick."

"So what?"

"Grandpa Frick...Mom's dad, right?"

Arnold looked puzzled. "Jeff, last I checked there are no more Fricks in town."

Jeff dropped the subject and visited with his brother and niece until dark.

It was an incredibly humid night; heat lightning lit up the sky and thunder rolled in from a distance. Jeff lay over his sticky sheets thinking about the conversation he had overheard the previous evening.

As he began to doze, the voices returned from the static of the monitor. The first voice seemed to be speaking German; he listened but couldn't make out any of the words. The second voice he thought he could make out: "Frick's up there rolling a fat cigar for Lester, and they're both laughing."

There was more jumbled conversation, but it was unintelligible and Georgia was stirring, likely due to the intermittent thunder. Jeff tended to his daughter and slept the rest of the night without incident.

The next morning, he dropped Georgia off with her mother's grandmother and visited the public library.

"Sir, can I help you find something?" asked the librarian. Jeff was digging through the microfiche cabinet in the town's history section, trying to find some information on the names 'Frick' and 'Lester'. He vaguely remembered hearing about them during elementary school lessons about the local factories.

"Yes, I'm searching for a man named 'Frick' who was associated with the Lester factory?" The librarian raised an eyebrow and nodded.

"Ah, I see. Francis Frick?" Jeff nodded. The woman went right to the Sun Newspaper file, pulled a microfiche and took him over to the reading machine.

"Francis Frick was the foreman that many of the tannery workers blamed for the fire of aught five." She scrolled to the newspaper article about the fire. He was surprised it was a small back-page notice and not a headline story.

"Is this it? Wasn't this big news?"

The librarian smirked. "Harry Lester not only owned the factory that burnt, he owned the newspapers, mills, stores, and he even built this library. He buried any investigation into whether or not Frick was culpable."

Jeff felt ashamed; he was pretty sure he was somehow related to this Frick guy. His mother's family had left the area long before she came back to study at the local university, where she had met his father.

"So, what *actually* happened?" asked Jeff.

"Alright, there's history as told by the people who've experienced it, and then there's the official town history that I'm paid to record and preserve," said the librarian. Jeff looked at her dumbly.

"Frick was one of Lester's factory foremen. He would lock the doors of the tannery during work hours. He himself paced the roof, chomping on cigars, while the men put in their ten to twelve hours in that hot stench below. A tannery in summer is possibly the worst smell a worker will ever experience." She paused, studying his face.

"Go on, please."

"Anyway, there was a fire and six men died. Those are facts; whether or not the doors were locked at the time is 'officially' disputed. There were enough exits, they were just locked..."

"So why did only six die?"

"Three brothers managed to pry two of the narrow windows open and are likely the reason why hundreds didn't die that day. Most of the men climbed out and were given enough time to do so by the trio, as well as three other workers who pulled men from tannery pits in the smoke."

Jeff's eyes went wide at the mention of three brothers. "So, Frick was protected by the owner and this was all swept under the rug?"

She nodded. "That wasn't the worst of it, either. Apparently, Frick was also charged with burying the bodies. They were immigrants and had no one to bury them, and he may have dumped them all in the same unmarked grave." Jeff bristled at the injustice of it all. The librarian continued, "Of course that last bit is pure speculation. There's no evidence of any of it after the facts that there was a factory fire, six men perished, and the doors were probably—more than likely—locked on orders from Frick."

"Is there any idea where they were buried?"

She seemed hesitant to continue beyond her role as professional historian. "Well, Lester owned the land that would become Valleyview Cemetery. If I were to guess, I'd say it's as good a spot as any."

Jeff thanked the woman and headed back home. He was really disturbed by the idea that there might be a mass grave in his figurative, or literal, backyard.

Days passed. Jeff took care of his daughter, went to work at his delivery job, and at night listened for voices over the monitor. After a week of nothing, he was frustrated and went to visit his brother.

"How you been, Jeff?" Jeff looked tired, Arnold was worried about him.

"Same old."

"You look like shit, man. What's up?"

Jeff screwed his lips, debating whether or not to tell Arnold that he had been investigating the voices he heard those two nights over his baby monitor. "Can I ask a favor?"

"Sure, Jeff." Arnold figured his brother was finally going to give in and come work for him.

"Can we use your GPR to search my backyard?" Arnold was incredulous. Jeff was asking to use his incredibly expensive ground-penetrating radar system.

"Fuck, no... Why?"

"I really think the grave of those workers who died in that factory fire might be in mom and dad's backyard."

Arnold shook his head. "I don't have the time, bro. Why would you even think that? And even if it were true, what are the chances it's in our little patch when the cemetery itself is so big?"

"Arnold, mom and dad's house is over 100 years old. It was given to them by mom's family..."

"So what?" Arnold asked.

"I think that guy Frick was the one who built it and lived in it."

"Jeff, sure, we are related in some way to that old story; sure, the house was a gift from the Fricks who live in Pennsylvania—but why would this guy bury bodies in his own backyard?"

Jeff did not have an answer for his brother. "I don't know—and I know this sounds more than crazy. But the baby monitor—it only has a range of about ninety feet and that cemetery fence is more than ninety feet away."

Arnold sighed, all too used to his brother's whims.

"Please, bro?"

"Shit. I guess I could bring the GPR over sometime this week. If only to show you, you're fucking crazy and need a girlfriend and/or a psychiatrist."

It was not quite 3 a.m. when Jeff was awakened by voices over the baby monitor.

"When Frick's grave has been made, we will make it still better."

"Cigar roller, butcher of men!" The voices seemed different to Jeff, much angrier.

"He lies with his fat wife above, laughing." All of the voices seemed to merge into one incomprehensible garble, while Jeff distinctly detected the stench of burnt hair. He had never been as frightened, save for the night he fell and broke his leg. He thought of how he lay in the cemetery propped up against a headstone, gritting his teeth in agony until his pals finally discovered him.

He got up and searched the house for the burning smell but came up short. It eventually faded and he was satisfied it was nothing to worry about.

Days and nights passed. Jeff had trouble sleeping but heard no more conversation among the dead. Finally, Arnold called him and said he would be over with the GPR. Jeff dropped his daughter off with the sitter and waited for his brother to arrive.

"Come out here and help me with this thing; it's heavy as hell." Arnold was at the front door. Jeff leapt from the couch and went out to help him lug the machine to the backyard.

"I hope you know this machine isn't going to give us a picture underground. We're not going to be able to see skeletons grinning back at us." Jeff nodded.

It was slow going. Arnold inched the machine along the ground for an hour before he said much of anything. Finally, he decided it was calibrated right to look for depressions within six to eight feet of the surface.

"As far as I know, there's only the one gas line back here, so that'll appear fairly often and be a good marker." The two men dragged the machine across the yard, back and forth, for hours. It was getting dark when Arnold decided they had collected enough information to analyze.

"Let's go inside and get a drink. The computer will take a few minutes to get us our radargram." They went in and set up shop on the kitchen table. Fifteen minutes passed before Arnold was able to study the information they had gathered the preceding hours.

"So, this is where that old tree stump was, here is the gas line, like I said, and... Oh, there's something."

Jeff grew anxious. "What, Arn?!"

Arnold grinned at him. "See these diffractors all grouped right here?" Jeff nodded. Arnold continued, "It looks like a big hole that was dug and filled in."

"That's it, then!" Jeff practically jumped out of his chair.

"Hold on. It just means that at some point a hole was dug there. I'd guess it was four feet deep and eight feet wide." They talked about it for a while. Arnold brushed off his brother's insistence that it was the mass grave of the tannery workers who died a century before.

"I can get us a backhoe. Let's dig it up and see."

Arnold shook his head. "Ha. Try getting a permit for that!" They went back and forth; Arnold was completely against digging.

"Tomorrow morning, I'm digging."

24

Arnold was worried about his brother's obsession. He left him to his thoughts and returned to his family.

That evening, after he put his daughter to bed, Jeff began digging by hand. He placed the baby monitor next to his electric lantern, on a wheelbarrow, so he could listen to his daughter's light breathing. He dug into the dirt at the spot his brother begrudgingly revealed to him before leaving.

Jeff dug for hours before he heard the voices over the monitor. He was sweating profusely and sat down in his shallow hole to listen.

"We won't mourn in the darkness." A second voice continued the thought, "while Frick sleeps sound above."

"Call the roller of big cigars. Frick, then Lester!" The German said his piece next but Jeff couldn't understand a thing, save for the angry, spiteful tone.

"We three brothers will make their graves." Jeff sat propped up against his dirt pile, and as he listened to the static, he nodded off into the warm August night.

Arnold rushed down the hill to his brother's house after receiving a call mid-morning at his office. Jeff hadn't dropped Georgia off at her grandmother's house and wasn't answering his home phone. She told him she had contacted the police.

When Arnold arrived, he rushed into the house and immediately heard the baby crying. He went to Georgia's room, picked her up, then looked for his brother throughout the house. Nothing. He returned to the baby's room to change her and grabbed an instant bottle of formula from the nursery cupboard. While he fed her, the sun's glint off the shovel in the backyard caught his eye. He saw Jeff's lantern next to the shovel and a smooth patch of dirt.

Arnold hurried out back with the baby and saw the monitor resting in the grass. He set the baby down as he grabbed the shovel and vigorously began digging at the grave. Minutes later, two police officers entered the backyard and yelled for Arnold to get on the ground. He kept digging until one officer tackled and handcuffed him, while the other grabbed the baby.

"My brother!" Arnold screamed at the cop to let him go so he could save Jeff. They put him in the squad car and gave Georgia to her grandmother when she arrived soon after. Arnold convinced the police to dig up the patch. They kept him in the car while they contacted the caretaker from the cemetery to help them remove the dirt.

Jeff died of asphyxiation in a shallow grave. His brother was not charged and was let go after hours of interrogation and a number of witnesses emerged to place Arnold at home or work during the preceding hours.

After Jeff was properly buried in the expanded northern parcel of Valleyview, well out of sight of the family home and backyard where he had been buried alive, Arnold paid for further excavation of the site by forensic anthropologists from the local university.

They spent days digging, plotting and planning before they found a mass grave about four feet below where Jeff had met his end. They could identify five to six different adult males. DNA testing showed that three of the unknowns were closely related. A memorial was erected in their honor and each was given a proper burial.

For more information on Frick and Lester, see Appendix A.

The Caretaker

Zeke Taylor slammed the door to his mom's rusty double-wide and ran off into the dusky December evening.

"Get back here, you little shit!" yelled Todd, his mom's boyfriend, as Zeke trucked it down the block. Todd was a mechanic at Barker Auto down on Harrison Drive. He had greasy, black hands, and had no problem using them to do realignment work on Zeke's face. His mother was always too hopped up on Oxy to notice.

Zeke ran and ran—out of Lestershire's dingy south side and into the well-manicured north. Todd would never look for him there; the bastard was too drunk to walk even fifty yards. He turned onto Memorial Drive and stopped in front of Valleyview Cemetery. He was sure no one would bother him there.

He walked through the front gate and up an eastern path. Grey, granite tombstones jutted out of the earth at odd angles in all directions. He passed row after row of graves. A man named Eric Bacon had been buried there in 1896. Some poor sap named Wintermute bit the dust in 1914. Baby Anthony, with his weathered lamb monument, died in 1934.

These were all just names, except for one grave, a relatively new one, located at Plot No. 47.

Her name was Ethel Taylor, but Zeke had always called her Baba. She was the one who watched him when mom was out with Rick or Steve, or Neil—the Wal-Mart cashier who smelled like a walking bottle of Jim Beam. She was the only one there for him at his middle school graduation or the Pinewood Derby or the first show of his punk rock band, Drowning Memories. When Baba had passed away the previous May, Zeke spent a week in his bedroom.

He took a pack of Camels out of the back pocket of his jeans, popped out a cigarette, and lit up. The orange glow of the filter looked like a floating flame in the deep, dark blue of the evening. He wandered through section 4D and looked at the headstones. Many of them were decorated with freshly cut flowers. The yellows and purples and reds of the bouquets stood out against the oh-so serious, gloomy headstones.

These people are worm-food and somebody still cares about them, thought Zeke. *I'm alive and don't even get a birthday card.* He plucked the cigarette from his mouth and rubbed it out on a nearby headstone.

Zeke took two steps away from his makeshift ashtray when a voice called out, "What the hell do you think you're doing?"

He felt a moment's panic at being discovered. The muscles from his stomach to his neck tightened. To his right, standing next to a mausoleum like a damn boogeyman, was an elderly man in baggy, denim overalls and a long, black overcoat. The old coot was short and stout, with a mouthful of ugly teeth and a headful of matted, white hair. He was covered head to toe in dirt.

"Nothing," said Zeke, sheepishly. He glanced over at the pack of cigarettes, which he had forgotten on top of the headstone. The man drew closer. He held a lantern up to his head, the glow of which cast nasty shadows across his cracked and wrinkled face. He smelled like he regularly bathed in unleaded gasoline.

"Don't lie to me," said the man. He nodded his head toward the cigarette butt lying in front of the headstone. "I'm the caretaker for this here cemetery. And nothing gets past me."

Zeke turned to walk away, but the man grabbed him by the arm. His grip was shockingly strong for a guy Zeke figured was closer to seventy.

28

"Where do you think you're going?!" hollered the seething senior, his rum-soaked breath warm on Zeke's face.

Zeke panicked and yanked his arm out of the old man's grasp, then sprinted toward the front gate.

After running fifty or so yards, he looked over his shoulder. He couldn't see the man anymore, but could make out the lantern glow—and it was definitely moving in his direction. He bolted out of the cemetery and headed for home, the thought of Todd's XL belt from earlier that evening still fresh on his mind.

Zeke got out of school the next day and, rather than head for Scoville Trailer Village, walked across town, back to Valleyview. His ass was still sore from Todd's belt and he wasn't up for any more "penance." Some folks might say that hanging out in a cemetery was creepy or weird, but for Zeke it meant peace and quiet. He just had to make sure he didn't run into that cantankerous caretaker.

He had swiped his mom's flask and made short shrift of the remaining Captain Morgan's. After downing half the flask, he chucked it at a hanging basket of flowers and moved onward. There was no sign of the caretaker, so he walked to his grandmother's grave.

Zeke stood in front of her tombstone and smiled. Baba had always been a giving woman. She never failed to bring him a present when she stopped by, despite her meager retirement from Lestershire General. He thought about the time she came over with a big box of his favorite snack: peanut brittle. He had opened it with glee and gave her a big hug in thanks. Later that night he found out Todd had eaten it all. When he complained, Todd simply backhanded him.

The memory sent Zeke into a rage, and he tore through the cemetery, kicking over freshly placed flowers, teddy bears and other knick-knacks left behind on loved ones' graves. He was about to punt a bouquet of flowers clear across section 4D when he heard a strange whistling, then spotted the caretaker heading in his direction.

Zeke quickly ducked behind a nearby grave. He didn't believe in ghosts or ghouls or any horseshit like that, but he *was* certainly scared of pissed-off drunks. The ground in front of the tombstone was cool and hard against his hands. The earth smelled like a mix of mold and formaldehyde. The smooth marble of Mr. Edward Burberry's headstone felt cold against his face.

He heard the caretaker's heavy footsteps on the hard, dead grass, just yards away, punctuated by an out-of-place whistling. The caretaker's tune reminded him of carousel music. As the sounds drew closer, Zeke's heart raced in anticipation of a beating if discovered.

Zeke got on all fours and crawled toward a nearby grave. He had made it five feet or so when he felt the force of a heavy work boot on his back and heard the caretaker's gravelly voice, made hoarse by decades of inhaling dirt: "What did I tell you about messing around in my cemetery?"

He lifted his boot up and Zeke rolled onto his back, a sharp rock digging into his spine. He thought about the corpses rotting away just feet below, and how close he was to joining their ranks.

"I see you've been busy," said the caretaker, who stood silhouetted against the moon like a werewolf with a big beer belly. "Now you're going to help me clean it all up or I'll make you sorry you ever stepped foot in here."

The man reached toward a now trembling Zeke. Before he could grab hold of him, Zeke rolled onto his stomach, pushed himself back to his feet and shot off toward the cemetery's front gate.

This time, he didn't bother looking back.

Zeke wasn't a bad kid at heart, but he had a knack for getting into trouble, like a dog has for chasing cars. The same pigheadedness that earned him three straight weeks in detention at Lestershire High led him back to Valleyview a week later for another night of alcohol-fueled revelry.

He climbed on top of altar-tombs and pissed off the side, drunk out of his gourd. He smoked a whole pack of Camels and blessed each headstone in row 120 with a ceremonial cigarette butt. He made Valleyview his own little playground, and he was too hammered to care about any damn caretaker. He waited for the old man to come out and scold him, to grab him and shake him like the little shit-for-brains he was, but there was no sign of him.

The sun dipped below the horizon and the moon took its place, shining down on the headstones and casting rectangles, squares, and cross-shaped shadows on the ground. The trees, black and gnarled, creaked in the breeze. Squirrels scurried to their homes. The moldy stink of the grass and sod was never more pungent.

The whiskey that Zeke had swiped from Todd's pickup was doing its job; Zeke stumbled around the cemetery grounds like a one-legged zombie, falling over stones and walking headfirst into low-hanging branches. The liquor was so potent, in fact, that he didn't see the open grave ten feet in front of him. He just kept moving forward. Five feet. Sluggish and dry-mouthed. Two. One. Too late.

He yowled as he half-fell into the hole. His fingers dug into the coarse, cold dirt. He scrambled for something solid to grab hold of as he slipped in—a rock, a tree root, anything. But the dirt crumbled through his shaking white knuckles like sand. He lost his grip completely and fell to the bottom of the hole, landing on the cold, rocky surface below. He hit the ground awkwardly, his ankle twisting beneath him at an unnatural angle. He screamed as he held his now useless appendage.

Zeke cried out for help, yelling at the top of his lungs for what seemed like hours. No one came. He was seven to eight feet below the ground in the middle of an empty cemetery on a cold, late autumn night. *Who the hell would come other than Death himself?* he thought. He attempted to stand up, holding onto the freshly dug earthen wall for leverage, but his leg was too mangled to hold any of his weight.

The temperature, already a frigid twenty degrees, was falling rapidly. He tucked his arms inside of his flannel shirt and curled up into a ball as flakes of snow began to fall into the dark pit. His teeth chattered like an automatic weapon; meanwhile, his body began gently shaking.

He gradually stopped fighting the cold and drifted into a dreamlike state. He remembered how Baba would hold him and tell him everything would be okay. Even if it wasn't going to be okay, he still *felt* better. But she couldn't help him now. She was well below the surface herself, boxed up and rotting away. No one was coming. He doubted his mom would even notice when he wasn't in his bed in the morning.

Another hour passed. His trembling body, which up to that point felt numb and cold, seemed to warm as he drifted. The snow began to fall harder and a small mound gathered up over his useless leg. *I'm going to die here*, thought Zeke. *That old, crotchety caretaker is going to find my body in the morning and they'll bury me three days from now. Hell, they might as well just throw the dirt back in this hole and call it a day.*

He was about to close his eyes and accept his fate when he heard a faint whistling. It was the caretaker. Zeke was in such bad shape that he contemplated yelling to him for help, but then he recalled their last meeting. He figured he had angered the old man enough that he would either laugh at him and let him learn his lesson the hard way—or worse—he might start shoveling the dirt back into the hole.

Crunching, heavy footsteps approached the grave. Zeke closed his eyes and held his breath as he shook violently in the frostbit cold. When the crunching stopped he opened one eye and slowly looked up. His heart jumped and he nearly fainted when he saw the overwhelming figure of the caretaker in silhouette, leaning over the hole, shovel in hand. He buried his head in his arm to hold back tears, resigned to whatever fate the caretaker deemed suitable.

"Grab my hand, kid!"

He looked up to see the caretaker kneeling at the edge of the grave, holding out his hand. Zeke hesitated, unsure if it was a trick, although ultimately he knew he had no choice, as he could no longer feel his fingertips or the foot attached to his swollen ankle. Not to mention, he still had a strong desire to not die in that hole.

Zeke slowly got up, supporting himself on his good leg. He held his hand out to the man in silhouette. With the strength that could only come from decades of hard labor, the caretaker pulled Zeke out of the hole and onto safe ground.

Zeke lay on the snowy grass, panting as the caretaker loomed over him.

"You could have gotten yourself killed," said the caretaker, who sounded more like a concerned parent than the deranged old man Zeke had thought him to be.

"Thank you...sir," said Zeke, trying to speak between the shivers.

The caretaker shook his head. "See what kind of shit you can get into, foolin' around in here at night? I don't want to see any more shenanigans from you, you hear?"

Zeke nodded. He was too shaken up to say anything intelligible. The caretaker nodded back and scratched his big belly. "Now let's get you out of here before you freeze to death."

He lifted Zeke up over his back and carried him to the front gate. A car approached and the old man set Zeke down on the sidewalk beneath the iron arch. Zeke hobbled toward the street and waved both arms at the already slowing vehicle. The driver stopped and got out to help the teen, as it was obvious how bad a shape he was in.

As the car drove away from the cemetery, Zeke looked out the passenger window, intending to wave goodbye to the caretaker. But the man was nowhere to be seen.

Months passed and the perpetual snow melted in Lestershire. Folks traded their blow-up, light-up, officially licensed Christmas decorations for bunnies, chicks, and Easter eggs. Zeke walked back into Valleyview Cemetery for the first time in months, sober and collected for a change.

The sun shined down on the rich, green grass. Blue skies and puffy, white clouds were reflected in the shiny, marble tombstones of sections A through G. Zeke saw an old man mowing the grass and walked toward him, thinking it was the caretaker. He wanted to thank him for saving his life. But when he drew closer, he saw that it wasn't the same man. This fella was taller, more svelte, and he was wearing khakis. Compared to the other caretaker, this guy looked like a damn Gap model.

Seeing Zeke approach, the man let go of the handle on the mower. The engine powered down and the cemetery was suddenly, appropriately, serene.

"Can I help you, young man?" said the stranger.

"Hi. I'm looking for the caretaker." said Zeke. "Have you seen him around? I owe him big time. He kind of saved my life a few months back."

The man gave Zeke a quizzical look. "Are you sure you're not thinking of someone else? I've been the caretaker here for roughly twenty years."

Did I dream all that up? thought Zeke. "Oh, I'm sorry," he said. "I just figured he was the caretaker. You know, the old guy with the white hair? Wears overalls and whistles old tunes?"

34

The middle-aged caretaker looked at Zeke like he had just told him he shaved cats for a living.

"That sounds a hell of a lot like Charlie Mathers. But he's been dead for a couple decades now. Gruff guy, but he was good at heart. Funny, that's just what killed him. Died of a heart attack in '79. I took over right after."

Zeke felt like his stomach had just floated up and lodged into his throat.

"You must be mistaken," said the man. "I'm the only guy here. I had one fella mowing the lawns, but I caught him sleeping on the job a few weeks ago. Had to fire him." He rolled his eyes.

"Yeah, maybe I'm thinking of somebody else," said Zeke, realizing the strange and mysterious truth of the matter. He started to walk away when the caretaker called out to him.

"Hey, you seem like a decent kid. You looking for a job? The grass is starting to get pretty high here, and I can't keep up with it all by myself. What do you say?"

Blades of grass shot up from the ground as Zeke made his way through section 4D of Valleyview Cemetery with a Husqvarna weed wacker.

He released his finger from the trigger and the machine shut down, the spinning line thwacking against the ground. Baba's grave had never looked so nice. She would be proud of him, as she always had been.

He turned and waved to Charlie, who was busy trimming the hedges in section A5. Charlie waved back and scratched his gut.

Zeke looked around the cemetery. It was a peaceful place. Even the moldy grass was starting to smell sweetly familiar.

A Matter of Course

My Apple iWatch says I'm on track to set a new PR. Ten minutes. Just through the cemetery, up the road, past the dental office and TV station, and then home. Let's go, Rick. Don't drag ass!

Rick Sellers stormed through Valleyview on his evening run. He had all the gear, the right $300 shoes, even a water bottle specifically molded to lock with his hand while he did his roadwork.

Caretaker better not even look my way tonight. I pay more in property taxes than he earns in a year. Idiot. As if I'm disturbing anyone or anything by running through this shithole.

Running through the cemetery was the most convenient path for him to loop back to his house at almost exactly five miles. He ran five miles six days a week. The caretaker had warned him about using the cemetery as his training ground more than once, and each time he had blown the guy off, pretending he couldn't hear him due to music in his earbuds.

Something caught Rick's eye and he paused. *Huh? I could've sworn that angel was facing the other way...*

He ran in place for a few seconds studying the large, granite statue, before he made his push up the tougher incline, toward the rear gate.

Crap! That damn angel could've cost me. Messed up my rhythm.

He finished his run through the cemetery and tread the winding road that led to his elite hilltop neighborhood.

Days later, while Rick was making the long climb through Valleyview, he came to an abrupt stop in front of the angel monument. The six-foot seraph on the cubic headstone had its arm raised and wings spread—he was certain its wings were flat, and its hands down and palms out the previous night. He walked toward the figure, weaving around various grave markers.

I'm sure this was the one I stopped at. Jason Bartlett 1980-2015. Why does that name sound familiar? Whatever. I'm sure I only noticed it because it's new and this is an old section I've run through a hundred times.

Rick continued on his run and was back home as the sun dipped below a far western hill. He showered, ate, and went to bed early.

The next morning, before work, he logged onto Facebook to kill some time.

Mom sent a message about her and Dad's next vacation. Should probably call her this year. People are sharing the typical articles, mostly political idiocy, plenty of whining. Yep, Facebook...Wait. What are they going on about? Someone from high school OD'ed? Not very surprising, seems to happen every other year. Huh? Jason Bartlett? He's friends with my ex? Do I still love him? Oh, Christ, I remember Bartlett now. Tall, goofy kid, definitely not Facebook friends. When did this happen? Read his headstone yesterday. Maybe they buried him last weekend.

His mouth hung open when he realized that Jason Bartlett died the night before. Rick being Rick, he did not dwell on the inconsistency of it for too long, and got to his office early, ready to take on the day.

Not even considering the nature of the previous evening's turn of events, Rick ran his normal route through Valleyview after work. He thought about the angel as he drew closer to it, although he did not think too hard—that is, until he saw that it now had both arms raised in the air. He ran over to the marker and studied the inscription: *Alvin Burnett. Born: 1949. Died: 2015.*

He bristled at the name. It belonged to his neighbor, someone he had seen that same morning as he fetched his paper from the front lawn. Rick was startled out of his trance by a loud, gruff voice.

"I thought I told you, this is private property—not your goddamn personal track!"

He startled, but quickly realized who was talking to him and waved the older guy off like he was one of his subordinates.

Rick returned home and thought about the stone angel and his neighbor. He heard a lawnmower roar to life across the street as if synchronously dependent on his thoughts. *He's over there now cutting the grass. I'll have a look out the window, just to make sure.*

He cracked the shades of his large front window and watched the older man pushing his mower back and forth over his plush lawn.

Al looks good for a guy pushing seventy. Maybe I'll go talk to him about who he's using for his hedges. College football star right there. I bet he could still hit like a freight train. Like I'm gonna go over there and casually mention I saw an angel over an inscription with his name and date of death. Nope. He'd probably slap me across the mouth. Forget this cemetery crap; time for a movie and bed.

Minutes before Rick's alarm sounded the following morning, he was awoken by the wail of an ambulance. *Aww, Christ! Don't tell me, Mrs. Wagner broke another hip. All the money she has, why not pay a full-time nurse's aide?*

He went downstairs, started his coffee and peered out the front window.

Oh. It's at Al's.

Rick ran to his toilet, puked out the knot in his stomach, and was about to call in sick to work when another neighbor, Mark, stopped by with news: Al had passed during the night. Mark was a surgeon and had been first on the scene, as Al's wife had actually called *him* before the ambulance. He figured it was likely a cardiac arrest and that Al had died in his sleep.

Rick almost told Mark about the angel and the inscription but stopped before he made a fool of himself.

Rick avoided Valleyview for months after Al's death. He joined the local health club to continue his exercise regimen. But given time and pride, it was not long before Rick considered returning to his old course, irrespective of soothsaying angels.

Coincidence is all. Al was old, had horrible eating habits, and got no exercise aside from pushing that lawnmower. A few bad dreams and false memories and I'm running on the treadmill at the club like a teenage girl. God.

He was determined to return to the road and the cemetery that night. It was all he thought about that day, and he got little work done. When he got home he put on his gear, iWatch, and new sneakers, and pumped himself up for his run.

Let's go, Sellers. Don't be a queen. Personal record day. Five miles with hills in twenty-eight minutes! Looks like rain. Who cares?

As the sky darkened, Rick blew down the road from his house and practically sprinted down the side streets that led into the valley. His watch told him he was well ahead of his typical pace as he passed under the ornate cast-iron entranceway of Valleyview.

I guess the treadmill wasn't all bad. I'm frickin' unstoppable today. Caretaker Dickhead's truck isn't in its normal spot. Won't have to listen to that bug today. The rain fell lightly on Rick's sweat-wicking shirt and pitter-pattered off his exposed thighs below his brief runners' shorts. The wet pavement was no match for his new, technologically advanced shoes, designed specifically to deal with adverse road conditions.

As Rick came upon the headstone grouping, just before the major incline to the top of the cemetery, he kept his head down, determined not to lose concentration. As he trudged through, his second wind kicking in, he caught sight of it out of the corner of his eye.

Jesus! He stopped cold in his tracks as rain began to beat down upon his head. The angel with the outspread wings that had given him pause so many times before was now seemingly slate black. Rick figured it was the dark skies that gave it a strange hue, so he jogged the twenty yards or so to get a better look, slightly trembling in the cold rain.

However, it was not the sky nor the rain that had darkened that statue. At the black angel's feet, he read a new inscription: *Rick Sellers. Born: 1983. Died: 2015.*

Rick dropped to his knees as the rain poured down around him. He began to weep when he noticed all of the other black angels atop grave markers, each with fresh inscriptions, dooming people he had known, loved, and even some he thought he'd long forgotten.

All Hallow's Eve

James and Alexis Savage hadn't been to the town's Halloween carnival in ages. In fact, they couldn't remember the last time they had even gone out as a couple. It was Alexis' idea. *Let's just give this a chance, okay? Spend a couple of hours together without biting each other's heads off?* She figured the carnival was as good a place as any to attempt a resuscitation of their marriage. The locals came out in droves and there was a cheeriness in the air that was practically contagious. Maybe, just maybe, that good spirit would rub off on James.

They walked into Greene Park and were immediately greeted by a giant scarecrow with a jack-o-lantern for a head. It had a twisted grin and pointed toward the main entrance to the carnival with a long, bony finger. Alexis looked at her husband and smiled. He got out his wallet to pay the ticket salesman.

"Eve-ning, folks," said the salesman, a bucktoothed yokel in caked-on vampire makeup. "Welcome to the Lester Harvest Fair!"

James handed the man a twenty. "Hi."

"So, are you two first-timers?" the salesman asked, a big, dumb grin on his face. He opened up the cash register and ripped off a pair of tickets from a big, orange roll.

"No," said Alexis. "We've been here before, six or seven years ago. Is there anything new we should check out?"

The salesman pointed across the street. "You've got to try the corn maze. It's huge and *really scary.* Been running three years now. Most popular attraction we got."

Alexis gave the man a puzzled look. "Across the street? You mean over in *the cemetery?*

"Yep. Starts at the gate and goes quite a way up the hill. Careful not to trip over any coffins!" They didn't even feign a smile at the vampire's attempt at a joke. He stamped their hands with a smiling pumpkin logo and James and Alexis walked into the fair.

Greene Park was aglow in orange and yellow lights. Cornhusks littered the ground, fences, game booths, and even some of the rides. Paper-mâché bats hung from a string, which led all the way from the basketball courts to the pavilion, where the 4H club was cooking up "hell dogs" and "monster burgers." Spooky sounds blared out of the speakers attached to the Little League field—rattling chains, creaking coffins, typical hokey stuff. The air was thick with the scents of apple cider and kettle corn.

"What do you say? Want to get a couple *monster burgers*?" asked Alexis playfully as they walked among the costumed denizens of Lestershire.

"I'm not hungry," said James.

"C'mon, we didn't even eat dinner. Are you sure?"

"Yeah, I'm sure. Don't *do* this."

Alexis looked at him quizzically. "Do what?"

"Hound me. We haven't even been here five minutes. Don't start."

"Hound you? I asked if you wanted a burger."

"And I said no. Should have stopped there." He started to walk away.

Alexis tugged at his arm. "Honey, okay. I'm sorry. How about a drink then?"

"Sure."

They walked over to the beer tent and James bought each of them a cup of pumpkin ale.

"S'good," he said in a disaffected tone.

"Yeah," said Alexis. "See, I told you this would be fun."

"Mmhmm," mumbled James.

An hour passed as James and Alexis knocked back a few beers each. The carnival became even trippier as the booze

43

began to take effect. They stumbled around, making fun of the various costumes and general attire of their neighbors.

"What a whore," commented Alexis, regarding a woman dressed up as a naughty witch with two kids in tow.

"Won't be long 'til she pops out another one, lookin' like that. But that's probably the point," said James. "I see them at my store with their EBT cards. They just keep breeding to get that monthly welfare increase."

"Oh my *god*, the *obesity*. I just want to knock that funnel cake out of that fat guy's hand." Alexis was louder than she intended and her target heard her dig. The large man with the pastry looked down at the ground in shame and hurried on his way.

"How about a game or something, dear?" asked James. He seemed to be in brighter spirits after the alcohol and came across as almost playful. Alexis played a few of the lottery-type games, he threw balls at stacked cans, and they even rode the Ferris wheel together.

Having had their fill of the fairground, they started back up the hill to the car, as sundown was less than an hour away. On their way to the parking lot, they heard a barker call out from the entrance of the corn maze, "Hey there, mister brave young man!"

James paused, curious how the old carny was going to try and sell such an attraction to two adults in their forties.

"Sir, madam—the most fun is certainly not in the park. Come have a go at my spook maze. I assure you, you won't be disappointed."

James chuckled and waved him off.

"There is a fear you might find, deep inside. Some laughs, too. Take your lady by the hand; she'll be trembling; you'll guide her through." The barker smiled wide. His wrinkled face and white mustache seemed to bring out the yellow in his tobacco-stained teeth.

"Let's do it, Jamey. It's still early." Alexis pulled gently on her husband's hand in the direction of the gate. He begrudgingly followed, unsure of how much fear, fun, or laughs they might find in a cornhusk labyrinth through the town cemetery.

"Yes, sir—this way, through the gate," the old man said, then continued, eerily, "Choose the right path and you'll go free, choose the wrong path and you might just *scream*."

James looked at Alexis, both smirking at the carny as they passed into the first husk corridor. Tall stalks, yellowed and dry, loomed over them as they walked the first stretch of the maze. The sweet aromas of the carnival were replaced by a sour stench, some pungent combination of mud, straw, and manure. There was just enough evening sun peering through the trees to still see down each pathway.

They turned the first corner and Alexis yelped. A large, pumpkin-headed man stood on the other side, wielding a chainsaw. Although it was held in the ground by a stake and its face was painted on, it still struck a frightful image. Its twisted smile was so lifelike, so artfully realistic, James had to do a double-take to make sure there really wasn't a deranged killer standing before them.

"That guy wasn't joking," said Alexis, gaining her composure. "They let *kids* in here?"

"They didn't have this kind of sick stuff when we were young. Worst they ever had was a half in the bag Wolfman or a cheesy Frankenstein monster. Got to give it to the artist that painted these faces, though."

They proceeded through the maze, getting lost, backtracking, finding their way, getting lost again. The further they ventured in, the more unsettling the scenes became. Every so often the maze would widen to accommodate various groupings of effigy, furniture, and props. They passed an execution scene. Pumpkin villagers were gathered around a guillotine. A headless man knelt next to it, his severed gourd a few feet away bearing a ghastly expression.

The next scene they came upon was so disturbing that Alexis clutched her husband by the arm and buried her face in his shoulder. Four pumpkin people sat around a table, holding forks in their hands. The artist had painted big, drooling tongues hanging out of their mouths and had somehow, with nothing more than cheap acrylic paint, captured a look of insane glee in their eyes. Set before them, dressed with gourds, corn husks, and other bounty of the harvest, was their feast— a pumpkin person with a horrible scream on its face. It's "body" was ripped open, hay and red ribbon coming out of its chest.

"This is sick," said James.

Alexis was repulsed. "What kind of a corn maze is this? I can't believe the town would approve something like this."

They continued through the maze. Ten minutes passed and the last cup of alcohol finally took effect. James pinched Alexis' butt and she turned around and laughed.

"Hey, mister, what do you think you're doing?"

James pushed her against the fence supporting the corn stalks and kissed her.

"Jamey, what if someone comes by?"

He unbuttoned her shirt. "We haven't seen anyone for a while. It's fine. Besides, it's getting pretty dark in here."

They continued, more clothing coming undone, more groping. The newly risen harvest moon shone through the colored leaves of a nearby oak.

They were in the middle of things when they were startled by a loud bullhorn.

"What was that?" asked Alexis, quickly covering her chest with her arms.

"I don't know," said James, lying. He knew it was the signal that the maze was closing; he'd read it earlier on a sign near

46

the ticket booth. He dragged her down to the ground behind a wooden sarcophagus and a rising mummy. Alexis' bare skin pressed into the cold, muddy, straw path as they made love.

James and Alexis dressed and continued through the maze with the exit in mind. It was twilight and already quite dark. The noise from the carnival had all but faded.

They walked and walked, but no matter how much they backtracked and re-routed, they could not find the exit.

"We already went this way!" cried Alexis.

James snapped back at her, a familiar bite to his tone. "I know that, Alexis. You think I'm trying to get us lost? Just calm down. We'll be out in no time and you'll be home in time for your Kardashian crap."

Alexis immediately regretted what they had done in the mud. "Don't talk to me like that!"

James looked at her with contempt. "I'm not doing this right now."

"I'm scared and I don't appreciate you being mean to me for no reason."

"Oh, c'mon. What are you afraid of? We're in a damn corn maze. We'll get out eventually, okay?"

"You know I don't like small spaces. I swear the path is getting narrower and narrower."

"Then why'd you push me to come in here? I was ready to leave and you insisted we do this."

Alexis was about to tear into her husband when she heard two voices ahead. "I hear somebody. Maybe they can help us get out of here."

They turned the corner and came upon another couple standing in the path. They looked to be about the same age. Alexis noticed that they were holding hands.

"Excuse me," said Alexis, walking up to the pair.

They turned and smiled. "Hello."

"My husband and I are lost, and we were wondering if you could help us get to the end of this thing." Alexis looked at James, who seemed upset that she had asked a couple of strangers how to get out of a kid's corn maze.

The man grinned. "That's what a maze is for—getting lost!" He snickered to himself. "We've been through a few times over the years. We know the way out. You can follow us. Name's Steve. This is my wife, Rose."

"I'm Alexis. This is my husband, James."

"Pleased to meet you," said Rose.

James and Alexis followed the couple through the maze, making small talk. The sky darkened. The moon and a little light from the street lamps lit the path, enough for them to see ahead maybe ten yards. James noted that the pipe organ music from the carousel in the park had long since ceased playing.

"It's crazy what they call kid's entertainment these days," said Alexis as they passed a scene of pumpkin people dressed up as a satanic cult, readying a sacrifice. "I'd never let *my* kid come in here."

"Oh, how old are your children?" asked Rose.

"We don't actually have kids," said James.

"No," Alexis added. "It didn't work out." She gave her husband *the look*.

"I'm sorry to hear that," said Steve.

"Sorry?" said James, chuckling. "I'm glad we never had kids. Just another expense we don't need. Being *married* is hard enough."

"I don't think James and I would do well with kids," said Alexis. "We're too independent."

Rose looked at them like they were from another planet. "Steve and I couldn't have children. We tried and tried though..." She trailed off, looking down at the husk-laden path.

Steve shared an equal measure of heartache with his wife. "We would have given anything to have kids. Modern medicine couldn't solve our issue, however. Now it's too late for us."

Steve halted the group at an intersection not ten paces later. "This is the way out. Straight ahead."

The foursome reached an end to the cornstalk corridors, and the straw paths thinned to a brown, dead grass. The air was noticeably chillier as a thick evening fog rolled in. Alexis thought she could make out the road and a dim streetlight as she walked behind Steve and Rose, but the fog concealed almost everything.

"Are you sure about this?" asked James. They reached a road, but James thought it strange they hadn't passed through any gate to get to it. "This doesn't look right. I thought the maze dumped you back onto Memorial Drive."

"This is right, folks," said Rose, a strange smile on her face. "Trust us."

"Yeah, James," said Alexis. "You don't know what you're talking about. Let's go." She pushed him past Steve and Rose, and onto the dimly lit road.

The fog was heavy, but as their eyes adjusted they recognized the desolate nature of their surroundings, and could tell that they were nowhere near the carnival. In fact, after only walking a few yards, they could no longer see where they had exited the cemetery—and their guides were gone.

"Steve—Rose?!" Alexis called out into the palpable air. "Where did they go?"

"I have no idea." James replied. The couple paused and looked in each direction anticipating the reappearance of their new friends. Nothing, no response, just dead silence.

"James, where are we?" Alexis' voice trembled.

"I'm not sure. We might be on the north side of the cemetery on that shoddy service road. They really went all out on that maze if it went all the way back here."

"It doesn't seem right, Jamey. There are no cars or sounds or anything."

James was about to blow a gasket. He knew she was terrified, but he was too. "Just shut up for a while, Alexis. We'll find our way back. Let's just follow this road, okay? It loops back down to Memorial Drive and the cemetery."

They walked, their eyes searching through the fog for any sign of life or civilization beyond an intermittent street lamp. Finally, they reached another road and followed it for some time before coming upon what James knew to be the western gate of the cemetery. There was no evidence of a corn maze.

They walked along the iron fence toward the main gate. No sign of anyone or anything beyond the first few rows of headstones. They continued to the eastern gate, where the maze had begun. Again, nothing. The couple crossed the street to where Greene Park should have been. Nothing. No tents, no rides, no sign that any fair had taken place—just more fog and an empty field.

Alexis screamed, her cries dissipating into a vast nothingness. "James, what's going on?! What's happening?!" She grabbed him, her arms shaking violently.

James had a blank, dead look on his face. "I don't know," he whispered as they wandered back toward the open gate of the graveyard.

It was then that they *did* see something. Other souls, just like them, wandering to and from the cemetery. Mutilated corpses from centuries past soon surrounded the pair—beckoning to them, welcoming them to their new purgatory.

* * *

Steve and Rose walked out of the maze and were struck by the glow of orange lights and the sweet smell of kettle corn. The

50

Lester Harvest Fair was teeming with lively, smiling faces, and they were happy to join their ranks.

"Look, Honey," said Rose. "They still have that same Ferris wheel!"

"Let's take a ride, for old time's sake," said Steve.

He took his wife by the hand and they walked into the fair for the first time in decades.

Knocking Back

Jack and Tim sat with their friends in the Lestershire High cafeteria. They were trying to impress a couple of cute girls with stories of their legend-tripping exploits. The Internet provided fodder for many excursions into the great upstate countryside and suburban wild, even stories of their own humble town and county.

"We found the boy's tomb in the cemetery up there with the window and everything. You couldn't see in. Just the fact that it actually existed was amazing. We hear legends, then go out and test them. You guys should come out with us sometime." Jack had his audience rapt.

"Yep, Jack and I've found old castles and abandoned resorts downstate—haunted houses that delivered and plenty of spots that were lame. You don't always hit it out of the park with these kinds of things." Tim was referring to the few haunted roadways and gravity hills they had visited that seemed more a waste of gas money than an adventure.

"Have you guys been to Valleyview yet?" Ron spoke up after half-listening to his pals chat with the girls about their kooky exploits.

Jack responded, "Of course, man. Everyone has. You sit on old Schwartz's tomb and wait to get pushed off. Me and Timmy practically sat there all night—two nights in a row—and nothing." The girls laughed.

Ron shook his head. "No, no. This one isn't on the Internet. I heard this from an older guy who's been cutting the grass there for years. You need to find Eunice's mausoleum—it's supposed to be plainer looking and sort of set into the hill. All you do is knock, wait, and she'll knock back." The boys were curious; the girls' interest was piqued.

"You've never been, Ron?"

"Nah, I drink and play ball on the weekends, dude." The girls giggled at Ron's jab at Jack and Tim's choice of weekend activity. Ron continued, "But my buddy said that he's done it and he's heard the knocking. He said once you hear it you better run, 'cause if you see Eunice in her current state of decay...let's say, it's not going to be good."

"Shit, Ron, we're down. Tonight we'll meet you at the gate and you help us find the spot."

One of the girls, Lisa, chimed in, "We want to go too, guys."

Tim had forgotten about his pursuit of Lisa in his excitement over a new legend to test. "Okay, me and Jack will pick you two up and we'll meet Ron outside the diner?" They all agreed.

The group met at the west end gate of the cemetery after dark, having left their cars in the nearby diner's parking lot. Ron, Jack, and Tim searched inscriptions on the large central grouping of mausoleums with their two flashlights while the girls trailed behind, chatting. Forty minutes into the search, Lisa's friend, Kim, was getting impatient and spoke up: "Are we just going to wander around in the dark all night?" Ron was worried he was going to look like an idiot if they didn't find this tomb.

"Give us another twenty minutes, ladies, we'll find it." Tim chatted with Kim while Lisa began looking with Jack and Ron. Not ten minutes passed when Lisa spotted something interesting.

"Guys, none of these are set in a hill...What about over there?" All eyes turned to where she was pointing. Set into the hillside, among a group of big pine trees, was a plain-looking concrete structure

"I think we've got something. Good eye, Lisa." They made the five-minute trek to the little knoll, which was surrounded by average-size gravestones.

"Not very impressive." Ron shined his flashlight on the name marker above the door. Sure enough, it read: 'Eunice D. Walsh.'

"There she is!" The five stood in the crisp autumnal air waiting for a volunteer.

"Well...Who's going to knock first?" asked Tim. The girls took two steps back.

"C'mon, Tim. Let's both knock." Ron backed up with the girls while Jack and Tim coolly stood at the iron door, which was partly rusted and representative of the shoddiness of the structure as a whole.

"On three?" Jack nodded. "One. Two. Three!" The two boys rapidly knocked on the door for a few seconds then quickly jogged back the ten yards to where the other three were standing. The five held their breath in the quiet, still night, waiting for the return knock.

They paused for two full minutes before Lisa started laughing. "Guess she's not home?" The kids chuckled, though Jack and Tim were visibly disappointed that they did not confront some unstoppable supernatural force that night.

On their way down the winding path they ran into two guys who were looking for Schwartz's mausoleum. Tim tried to dissuade them from their pursuit.

"Nah, that's a dumb old story, guys. Everyone's done that and had a laugh. There's a mausoleum way up in the pines, set in the hill with a rusty door. You go up there and knock on Eunice's crypt and she'll knock back." Tim was having some fun with these two guys from out of town, who, like them, had found the story of Schwartz's Ghost on the Internet.

"You guys were just up there? She knocked back?" The five nodded in unison, saying how scared they were and adding other embellishments. The two newcomers were excited at the prospect and hurried up the path toward the pines. Tim,

54

Jack, and their friends left the cemetery laughing at the gullible guys and ate a late breakfast at the town diner.

The next day at school the five joked about their fruitless cemetery expedition. Ron said he had spoken to the guy who told him the story on Facebook when he got home.

"My brother's buddy, Z., he said you have to go way late, like after two and you have to say, 'Eunice, can you hear us?' and then knock." Kim and Lisa rolled their eyes and giggled at the corny addition to the story.

"Alright, I'm down," said Tim.

He and Jack were ready to go again that Friday night. Kim was the first to say she had no interest. Ron had an away football game so he was out. Lisa thought about it for a few minutes before agreeing to go with Tim and Jack. She liked Tim and was hoping he would eventually ask her to go somewhere more normal with him.

Tim, Jack, and Lisa hung out at Tim's house watching movies until midnight, then went down the road to the diner to eat before their cemetery sojourn. It was colder than their previous expedition just a few nights before. Soon enough, they were hurrying along the path up the cemetery hill to the pines and the knoll that hid Eunice's door.

"Lisa, you get to knock this time." The three again anxiously waited in front of the crypt, even though they had been disappointed only a few nights before in the same spot.

"Only if Tim knocks with me." He smiled at her and they stepped forward.

"Wait! Someone has to ask Eunice if she can hear us." Lisa jumped at Jack's interjection just as she was about to knock.

"Eunice, can you hear us? We've come to let you out." Tim looked back at Jack, happy with his little addition to the lore. They counted down from three and the pair knocked furiously at the door for more than a few seconds then backed off and waited.

After a long pause, they heard it. A muffled knocking seemingly from the other side of the door. When the knocking grew louder and more erratic, the kids bristled. Lisa gasped and hung onto Tim, and the three turned and flew down the hill until they exited the gate.

"Goosebumps; look." Jack showed them his arms while they panted from their exertion in the diner parking lot.

"I frickin' can't believe it." Lisa looked excitedly at a grinning Tim.

"And that, Lisa, is why we do these little trips."

The guys dropped Lisa off at her house and stayed the night at Jack's, talking until sun-up about their night. They slept for most of Saturday and ate a long breakfast mid-afternoon. Ron was the first person they messaged about their night. Of course, he did not buy their story, as he knew how these stories grew to be popular in the first place. Jack and Tim were already planning on returning that night for another go.

"What you think happened, man?" While Tim wholeheartedly believed in ghosts and all the things they explored, Jack liked to think of rational explanations for the stories he sought to experience firsthand.

"I guess someone could've been messing with us. Or, ghosts, zombies, you know..." replied Tim, who didn't think too hard about it, really.

"You said the door seemed looser the second night, like when you knocked it might have only been held by a small bolt lock?" Tim nodded, unsure what his friend was getting at.

"Tonight, we have to open that door, dude."

Tim knew his friend was serious. "I'm a lot of things, Jack, but I'm not a cemetery vandal."

"I think we could nudge it open a bit and get a peek inside, not really break anything." They went back and forth for some time until Jack more or less bullied Tim into agreeing to try and pry the door open, if only a crack.

56

Before the pair left for the cemetery, Tim had a long conversation with Lisa on Facebook about the previous night and even made an actual date with her for the following weekend. Jack and Tim played video games, researched other stories for future legend trips and just killed time until they could go back to the cemetery once more.

When Jack put screwdrivers and a crowbar into his backpack, Tim stopped him and questioned his motives. "We're not desecrating someone's tomb, Jack."

"Of course not, buddy. We've been on all these adventures together. When have I ever been a vandal?" Jack was right, Tim had never seen him purposely destroy anything on all their trips together. But it was driving Jack mad that he had finally come into contact with a legend that turned out to be true, and he wanted some bit of evidence. He was not thinking as clearly as the time they explored the underground tunnels and he'd insisted they turn back at the sight of a mutilated cat.

It was uncharacteristically dark in the cemetery that night as Jack and Tim walked the winding path toward their destination among the pines. There was no moon, and for whatever reason most of the streetlights on Memorial Drive that usually cast a faint glow upon most of the cemetery were out. Even the diner had been closed; the sign read 'for repairs.'

Tim shone his flashlight on Eunice's lonely tomb as Jack unpacked the tools. First, he twisted the handle and nudged the door. Tim was right about it being loose, and it almost seemed like he could just break the lock with little effort.

"The top of the door. I think we could bend it in." Tim pushed the top corner of the door while Jack crowbarred the growing crevice. They struggled at the door for a few minutes before it became clear their idea was not going to pan out.

"God, it's almost like I could just open the door, the lock is so loose." Jack shimmied the handle on the slim, rusted metal door. When he was about to give up and go back to his tools, the door popped open nearly six inches and came to a dead halt.

"Holy shit!" Tim looked at Jack. They were both smiling ear to ear.

"And we didn't have to break anything. I think there's something blocking the way. Help me push the door." The pair pushed at the bottom of the door so it was open about eight inches, which gave them enough room to peek inside with their flashlights.

Tim was the first to peer in at the shoddy concrete insides. There was nothing ornate from what he could see.

"Doesn't look like much. I guess there could be coffins in the walls, but I don't see any markers inside." Jack pulled Tim back so he could look in. He saw the same white, seemingly blank wall, and noticed something on the dirt floor, just behind the door.

"Let's get it open more so we can see what's blocking it." They pushed harder, it felt like sandbags weighing on the other side. There was enough room so they could both squeeze in. They were nervous and excited as they entered the dusty crypt, kicking up a cloud of dirt as they shuffled in.

"What is that?" Jack bent down in the dust shining his flashlight on a form and gasped.

"It's a body!" The dust settled enough that they noticed a second body slumped partly beneath the first. When they nervously shifted the first to see the second, it fell against the door, shutting it. They didn't notice the door close due to their shocking discovery of the two corpses.

"Oh hell, Jack—I think it's those two guys from last week!" The flashlights shone on the sunken, pale-gray faces and Jack too recognized the gullible legend trippers from their first trip to Eunice's mausoleum.

"Christ, they must've gotten stuck in here. We have to call the cops." Tim and Jeff looked at each other with the same horrific thought and lunged for the crypt door.

"Goddammit, it's stuck!" Jack and Tim fought the door with just their hands, attempting different methods of prying it open. Jack had left the bag with his cell phone and tools outside so he could fit through the crack. The door seemed firmer, not loose or shaky at all from the inside.

The pair took turns screaming for several days. Eventually, dehydration reached the point where they could no longer even speak to each other.

*   *   *

That following Tuesday, Ron brought Lisa back up to the tomb in the hillside so she could show him what she, Jack, and Tim had witnessed.

"C'mon, Lisa, I know you're messing with me." They had not seen Jack nor Tim at school and Lisa kept insisting they had heard Eunice knock back. "In fact, I'd bet you anything we won't hear a knock." She smiled.

"How about the loser buys dinner then?"

"I'll take that bet."

They took their places in front of the rusty metal door and excitedly knocked. After a brief pause they heard a faint knocking and then a louder more haphazard pounding. They bolted away from the haunted mausoleum, screaming and laughing.

Slumped against the other side of the door, Jack and Tim expended the last of their energy answering the knock, hoping someone would hear and rescue them before they took their final breath.

Out to Lunch

Mark Hurley was morbidly obese. He had been warned by his doctor of the risks and complications of carrying so much weight, specifically the likelihood of heart disease and organ failure. But the same could be said of millions of other folks who know that what they are doing is a path to death—they either do not care or are unwilling to tackle their vice.

The Broadview Diner served Mark each weekday during his lunch break: two double burgers with French fries and two sodas. The other regulars sometimes eyed him accusingly; some of the waitresses almost seemed to feel complicit in his gluttony. Mark was a nice enough guy, tipped decent, and no one ever said a thing to him about his habits—at the diner, anyway.

The reason Mark even became a regular at the diner was because his coworkers' lips were getting looser regarding his size and midday intake. He was becoming more anxious at the longer stares at the diner and knew it was only a matter of time. His anxiety fueled his eating habits and Mark had concocted a new routine to feed his turmoil.

"Hey, Mark—the regular?" Annie, like most of the waitresses at the diner, knew Mark's order, but this time he shook his head.

"Annie, I told my pals at work how much I love your guys' burgers and fries. I'll take four double burgers, four French fries, two regular and two diet sodas, please—to go." The waitress smiled and went off to put in his order. Mark was always nervous lying, and he knew his face was red just from telling this small fib.

The woman returned with two bags of greasy diner fare and a drink carrier for his sodas, and Mark was on his way. He had thought about eating in his car, but he worked close by and did not want someone he knew to catch him wolfing down his food in embarrassment. He had never been in the cemetery before and had driven by so many times, it just came to him that morning; he could eat exactly what he wanted in peace and quiet without the world's judgment coming down on him.

Mark tossed the two diet drinks in a small garbage can on the sidewalk before he slipped passed the west gate of Valleyview Cemetery. He certainly did not need four sodas, especially of the watered-down, diet variety. The sun was out, but it was not much more than seventy degrees, just about perfect for a shady picnic under a group of poplars. Mark ate his volume of burgers and fries, finished his sodas, and was back to work before his hour break was up.

This behavior, cemetery dining, continued for weeks and Mark became comfortable with his program. He had small hiding places to sit down and picnic in if there were a funeral or a jogger, or general activity in the cemetery. He had even found a perfect little marble overhang that kept him dry during a particularly bad spring rain.

One lunch break, a newer colleague, Dave, insinuated himself into Mark's routine. Mark had been telling Dave of the great burgers at the diner, and Dave wanted to have lunch with him. Mark tried to get out of the obligation as the hour drew near, but Dave was polite and seemed to really want to make a friend. Mark was low on friends, so he reluctantly agreed.

When the pair walked into the diner together, Mark was sweating profusely.

"Hey, Mark," said Annie. "You guys getting double burgers?"

"Yes, the usual, please. Dave here can't wait." Mark and the waitress shared a knowing look. He was trying to play it cool as if Dave was one of the guys he had regularly gotten lunch for. When the waitress returned with greasy bags and drinks Dave torpedoed Mark's story.

"Mark says the food here is really great. I've been wondering where he disappears to each lunch break." Dave was not trying to embarrass Mark, but Mark certainly turned a shade of red that screamed of embarrassment. He grabbed the food and nudged Dave out the door.

"Back to the office then?" Dave thought they would just eat at the diner.

"Nah, it's such a nice day. I'll show you the spot." Mark led the way into the cemetery. He brought Dave right over to his shade trees and sat down in the lush grass.

"Eat in the cemetery?" Dave was put off by the surroundings but did not want to hurt his coworker's feelings, especially after he had picked up on the bigger man's discomfort back at the diner.

The pair ate their food, split evenly between them, and made little small talk. Dave practically wolfed his down just so he could leave the creepy environs and his awkward, obese pal. When Dave left, Mark was mortified to think that he would tell everybody back at work what had transpired—the encounter in the diner, worst of all, Mark's regular picnic spot.

He was still hungry, having only eaten half his normal lunch. And thinking about the prying, judging eyes waiting for him back at the office made things so much worse. He dug through the bottom of the paper bag hoping for errant French fries; nothing but napkins and wrappers came of his search. Mark momentarily considered grabbing another quick burger.

He sprawled back on the grass and picked at weeds and dandelions. As he plucked at the yellow flowers he absentmindedly put the stem of one in his mouth. *Not bad*, he thought. He chewed the head of a dandelion for a few seconds and spit it out. *Yuck!*

Mark sat up and looked around at the surrounding graves. Some had wilting flowers and one looked like it had an arrangement placed that morning. He crawled the ten or so feet to the nearby flowers and popped a few into his mouth. *Terrible. Like the dandelion. Disgusting.*

The third variety of flower he tried was an orange lily that had just begun sprouting among the headstones. It was edible and Mark thought it quite tasty, consuming each of the five or six orange lilies he plucked from the ground around a particularly weathered stone.

It was hard returning to work. Dave had told a few of his coworkers what had transpired, and Mark knew they were snickering behind his back and judging him. What made matters worse was that he was incredibly gassy all afternoon. His flatulence was far from floral. A girl in an adjacent cubicle even gagged and asked to be moved due to his stench.

The following days, Mark's habit of eating away his feelings only worsened. His lunch hour in the cemetery became longer and longer, as he would seek out the orange lilies that seemed to be sprouting up all over. He was in deep with his boss, as he was always running late and stinking up the office. He lay in the grass and happily passed gas as he munched on lilies.

One day, when Mark was two hours late following lunch, his supervisor asked Dave to show him Mark's favorite midday hideout so he could confront him. The men made the short walk down Memorial Drive, past the diner and into the cemetery. They were overtaken by all of the orange everywhere. It looked like a field planted with one type of flower—just a blanket of lilies covering everywhere that was not already asphalt, marble, or concrete.

"Isn't there a caretaker?" asked Mark and Dave's boss. They were amazed at the unkempt scene before them.

"I must not have noticed them earlier in the week." Dave was shocked at the change in scenery from Monday to Friday.

He led his boss to the shady poplars and the mass of marble and granite that concealed Mark's preferred picnicking area.

They smelled the stench well before they reached their destination. It was notoriously Mark's—a sulfuric, rotting meat odor, mixed with the slightest of floral scents. The duo held their pocket squares over their noses as they battled the foul smell and navigated the shrubbery and various grave markers.

"What in God's name?!" screamed Mark's boss at the sight of a burst, bloated abdomen. Mark's stomach and intestines had torn his belly open like an overinflated balloon. The two men began gagging and puking at the scene. Flies had already begun swarming, gorging, and laying their eggs in his exposed innards. The sun beat down on that extraordinarily warm spring afternoon, making matters (and the smell) far worse.

Dave spoke for a few minutes with the paramedics when they arrived. He told them how Mark often ate his lunch in the peace and quiet of Valleyview. Mark was clutching a handful of orange lilies where they found him, and the paramedics asked Dave if Mark had eaten any of them. He responded that he didn't know.

The paramedics contacted a local botanist to identify the flowers and she arrived within the hour.

"So many flowers are poisonous and shouldn't be ingested. These almost look like the daylily, which is edible, but no—this variety had to have been planted here. It's indigenous to Central America and incredibly rare."

Scry the Crow

Amanda Clegg had a very troubled son. He had quit school and barricaded himself in his room for weeks before madness took hold and seemingly manifested itself in the form of demonic possession. Doctors had no answer for his sudden change in behavior and recommended institutionalization.

Amanda's husband and parents were gone. Her siblings lived across the country. It had been just the two of them in that little house at the edge of the park. She was sure a father figure was what her son needed to set him back on the right path. She was at her wit's end when she begged her parish priest to meet with her son.

Young Father Falco was one of the last to graduate a North American seminary school with a specialization in exorcism. He came to the house with his deacons and performed the ritual to no avail; the boy's condition only worsened. The priest continued to meet with the teenager, day by day and week by week, until they ultimately disappeared together late one night.

The police and the local Catholic parish were of little help. Her son was seventeen and left of his own sound mind and body—according to the police, anyway. The monsignor and his staff wanted to keep the issue quiet and told Mrs. Clegg they'd sent out their own investigators to look for the pair.

In the weeks following her son's disappearance she hired a private investigator, Jerry Javitz, to locate him. Jerry had updated her periodically, for months, before he ceased communication. During this time Amanda was wracked with guilt, fear, and depression, and even attempted to find her son herself—venturing into the seedy underbellies of nearby towns and cities

The following is the final letter Amanda received before the private eye himself vanished:

January 8, 1974

Dear Mrs. Clegg,

I've found your son. He's living not quite twenty minutes from your front door. Over the past six months I've tracked him from Chenango to Oxnard to Itaska, and finally to Lestershire. The heretical priest is still with him, along with two older women. There may be more who've joined the group since.

I would like to share as many of the details of his and my wanderings as I've time for. I'm not in the area, actually far from it. I'm sorry I couldn't convey this information to you in person. You'll come to understand why I fear for my safety.

I picked up his trail from the bar he frequented in Chenango. The barman heard he was headed north on Route 12, so I followed him from town to town, gas station to gas station, and plenty of folks remembered the priest and specifically your son's hands. He again bears the stigmata.

The sheriff near Oxnard was looking for the pair and questioned me when I came to town. Two of their farm cemeteries had been vandalized; the second apparently held what they were looking for. I found the small tomb they desecrated. It bore a window which they broke; and the deputy at the scene told me they had taken a young boy's skull. For what purpose, I still have no answer.

After the Oxnard sighting, I could find only bits and pieces of information regarding them. At some point, two older women, sisters apparently, joined your son and the priest. I'm assuming in Itaska, as they were living through the fall and early winter in an abandoned Methodist church on the river.

In that chapel I found a journal full of Indian script and some black books in English, the contents of which I won't disturb you with. I was able to secure translation of the Indian text at moral and spiritual cost to the translator. It was essential in locating your son and how I was able to find his current quarters.

In the forest, northeast of the cemetery in Lestershire, there is a small shack. I came upon it only by accident as I was tracking their coming and going from the graveyard. I staked out the small clan for weeks before I witnessed their purpose. The following is as accurate as I can describe and interpret from my own eyewitness account.

The priest only seemed to assist your son, who was constantly in a state of possession. They kept a number of caged crows for a very specific task. The priest would remove a crow, break its neck, and drop it in its throes. Your son seemed to be reading something of the crow's movements or its final resting state— thereby the group would wait for him to speak in tongues. The language I can only assume is Indian.

This would go on until nightfall, when they moved their dark ritual to a corner of the cemetery, repeating the crow sacrifice and scrying. Eventually, they took over a concrete mausoleum with a rusted green door to continue their black mass. When during the day I attempted to enter the structure, the two women (whom I did not see standing watch in the tree line) attacked me with long knives.

I was stabbed in my right leg and received stitches to both of my hands at the local clinic. Mrs. Clegg, they knew me by name. They knew I had been following them from the very beginning. Your son is not a seventeen-year-old boy. There's something much older about the way he speaks, something Indian in him. The priest isn't directing him as we originally thought. Your son, Mrs. Clegg, is gathering followers—for what purpose I cannot begin to guess.

Sincerely,
Jerome Javitz, P.I.

See *Appendix B* for more information.

Vermin

It was late afternoon on a hot summer day when Clyde Neely pulled his 1955 Ford pickup off Memorial Drive and into Valleyview Cemetery. His partner, Darryl Pook, sat next to him, drinking a Coca-Cola and bobbing his head to a new song by Johnny Cash playing on the radio. Darryl's younger cousin, Seth, sat between them, talking their ears off about some blonde with a nice pair.

Clyde parked the truck along the eastern fence. They got out and each pulled a shovel from the truck bed. The new plot was up a gravel path, and they would have to walk the rest of the way.

"I tell you, she looked like Marilyn Monroe's long-lost twin sister," said Seth. He ran his hand through his ginger hair. "Walking down Main Street like she just walked off a movie set. Oh, man, you should have seen her. *Woo-wee*."

"You're full of shit," said Darryl, shaking his head. "*No* woman in *Lestershire* looks half that good."

"Let's get a move on it, guys." said Clyde. "Parker wasn't pleased about the last job. Said it was messy."

"Parker can lick my boot," said Darryl as they arrived at the marked plot. "Cheap bastard. Always making us work overtime. I'm getting tired of it."

Seth, who couldn't work five minutes without smoking a cigarette or leaning on a fence post, nodded in agreement. "All Parker does is sit in that office of his all day—flogging his log, probably—while we slave away out here."

"Are you two tired of eating? 'Cause you won't be doing much of it if you keep slacking off. Now, *dig*." Clyde broke the ground, picked up a pile of dirt, and tossed it over his shoulder.

"I could go back to mowing lawns. Easy work," said Darryl.

"Yeah, and get paid jack shit," said Clyde. His shirt was already dusted with earth. "Cemeteries don't bother me none. I don't believe in ghosts or ghouls or any of that kid shit. Thing I do mind is missing out on a day's pay."

He shot Darryl a serious look, and his partner started digging.

Seth walked over with his shovel, already blabbering away. "You ever think about the bodies rotting away under here? All those worms crawling in and out of their noses and..."

"Shut up!" Darryl gave his cousin a good whack on the shoulder, and the kid got to digging.

A couple hours passed. The sun hung high in the summer sky, and the men baked in that hole, which had grown four feet deep.

"Gentlemen!"

They looked up to see Parker, the caretaker, standing over the hole. He was a big, burly man with a buzz cut, beady eyes, and a permanent scowl. His dog, Hooch, a St. Bernard, was sitting next to him, a nasty, pink tongue hanging out of his mouth.

"Good afternoon, Parker," said Clyde.

"Floral Nursing Home had three deaths in the last two days, and we have the special privilege of burying all of the bodies here at Valleyview. In order to accommodate this unusually large number of burials, I'm going to need you three to work overtime tonight. I need the holes dug by sunrise. You got it?"

Darryl plunged his shovel into the dirt. "Three plots by tomorrow morning? Sam hell, Parker, that'll take us all night! We're only halfway done with the first one."

"It might," said Parker, a tiny smirk on his face. "But if you want to work for me again, you'll do it."

71

"I don't got to put up with this," said Seth. "Murphy's Deli is hiring clerks, and I heard they treat their employees real nice. Even let them take home a pound of meat a week."

Parker smirked, the expression of a man who knows he has the upper hand. "Is that right? Well, maybe you boys ought to pile up in that rust bucket truck of yours and go ask Bill Murphy for a job."

Clyde quickly stepped in front of Darryl and Seth. "It's fine. My partners have just gotten too much sun. We'll have this done well before morning, Mr. Parker."

"Good," said Parker. He patted Hooch on the head. "Make sure it looks clean, too. I don't want any beer bottles or shit lying around like last time."

"Of course," said Clyde, giving his pals a sideways glance.

"And if you see any squirrels running around here, you have my permission to kill 'em. Little vermin run around chewing up flowers and pulling up flags. Took out four with my shotgun just this week." He walked back to his office, Hooch at his side.

Darryl spit in Parker's direction. "Son of a bitch. He's crazy if he thinks we can get this done in time. We really will be here all night."

Seth dug his shovel into the ground and leaned on the handle. "Takes at least four or five hours to dig a decent hole. I ain't that good at math, but there's no way we can get this done on time. They'll have to toss the rest of the bodies in the Quee-Hanna and call it a day."

Clyde pretended he didn't hear Seth. "Listen, if we work fast and don't bullshit, we can get out of here before midnight. Alright? Get home and maybe even have some time to make it with the wife."

Darryl laughed. "Yeah, right."

"And what the hell is he talking about with *squirrels*?" said Seth.

Darryl shook his head. "Who knows. Guy's a little *nuts*, yuk-yuk."

"Now, c'mon. Let's get back to work," said Clyde. "Time's a-wastin'."

They dug, and they dug some more. With each foot of dirt they uncovered, the sun traveled an interminable distance westward. Around 8:30 p.m. Seth went back to the truck to get the oil lantern.

They were talking about whether or not the Yankees would make it back to the World Series—Seth was yammering on about his god-awful Mets—when they heard a long howl off in the distance.

Seth gave Darryl a worried look.

"Coyotes," said Darryl.

"Coyotes?!"

"You get used to hearing them out here. Don't piss your pants."

"I'm not afraid of any coyotes," said Seth. "I'll tell you though, I've heard some strange things about this place. Don Barker, guy washes windows down on Taft, told me some wild story about his dad. Gave me the spooks."

Clyde rolled his eyes at Darryl.

"Don said his dad was out here one evening, years ago, tending to his mother's grave, when he sees a crazy looking guy run out of the forest. When the guy got closer, he could see it was an Indian—looking like he was straight out of *Gunsmoke*. He couldn't believe his own eyes 'til he saw the long knife in the Indian's hand. His dad ran right out of the cemetery and lived to tell the tale."

"Geez, Seth, did he have a bow and arrow too? Was his name Tonto?" Darryl chuckled.

"Go ahead and laugh. But I tell you, this place is—" Seth paused as another howl echoed throughout the cemetery. Not two seconds later, what sounded like a whole pack of coyotes was crying out to the moonlight.

"Let's just get back to work, alright?" said Clyde.

They dug another half a foot down when they heard another sound. But it was no coyote. It was a subtle little *Skreek-skreek-skreek-skreek*, and it was coming from within the cemetery.

"Hey, did you hear that?" asked Darryl.

"Yeah. It's probably a mouse or something," said Clyde. He was dripping with sweat.

Screek-screek-skreeeeeeek.

"That doesn't sound like any mouse I've ever heard," said Seth. "Sounds more like a rat. You should see the ones they got in those New York subways. Some the size of a small dog."

"Quit yapping," said Clyde, as he leered at Darryl's numbskull cousin. "It's a damn mouse. Get back to work."

They dug for another half hour. The *skreek* returned every few minutes, but they ignored it and kept to their task.

The lantern went dark and Seth climbed out of the hole to get more oil. "Christ. I could be out right now with Rebecca Donaldson, making it in her daddy's T-bird. Instead I'm out digging a hole for some stiff old ladies."

Clyde looked at Darryl and shook his head. "That kid ever shut up?"

"No, not since we were kids," said Darryl.

Clyde and Darryl dug for a few more minutes, clearing away another quarter foot of dirt, when they realized Seth had been gone for twice as long as he should have been.

"Seth—what are you doing up there?" called out Darryl. There was no response.

"Hey, kid, quit screwing around!" He suddenly remembered the flask sitting in the glove compartment of his truck. "You *better* not be drinking any of my whiskey!"

But Seth didn't reply. Clyde and Darryl listened intently but could only hear the sound of crickets and the light summer breeze blowing over the cemetery grass.

"Goddammit," said Clyde. "We're not going to get shit done without that lantern. *Seth, get the hell back here!"*

An eruption of coyotes howled, seemingly in response to Clyde's yelling. Clyde and Darryl paused, staring at each other.

"I'll go get him," said Darryl, a familiar annoyance to his tone. He stuck his head out of the hole to see if he could see Seth but immediately pulled it back down. "Holy shit!"

"What?!" said Clyde.

"Some crazy lookin' critter was rushing toward me— straight at my head. I think it was a squirrel. It had *red* eyes."

Clyde laughed hysterically, even paused his work for half a minute. "Are you kidding me? A red-eyed squirrel? Are you *on* something? Smoking dope like one of those beatniks now?"

"I'm not kidding. Damn thing darted toward me. I'm not joking. Look up there and see for yourself if you don't believe me."

Clyde put down his shovel and mockingly tip-toed over to the side of the hole. He made a big scaredy-cat face to Darryl and slowly lifted his head out of the grave.

The cemetery had grown several shades darker since he last climbed out to relieve himself an hour prior. From his position, he could make out a few rows of graves and a big oak tree. No red-eyed squirrels, though.

He turned back to Darryl. "I don't see shit. Especially not your idiot cousin."

"I'm not lying, man. Craziest looking thing I've ever seen."

Skreek-skreek-skreeeeeeeek!

Clyde popped his head back up to investigate the sound, and a flash of brown and white leapt toward him. He screamed as the thing landed on his face and sunk its tiny, razor-sharp teeth into his cheek. He fell backward into the hole as the creature—a squirrel with horrible red eyes—gnawed on his flesh.

Darryl scrambled over to Clyde and yanked the squirrel off his head. A mouthful of skin came off with it, followed by spurts of blood that seemed to fall in rhythm with Clyde's screams.

Darryl held the squirrel by its tail, its body gyrating and whipping back and forth like a 10-pound bass caught on a fishing line.

Skreek-skreek-skee-skee-skreeeeeeeek!

"Jesus Christ!" As fast as he could, he flung the squirrel against the side of the dirt hole and brought his shovel down on its head. The squirrel flattened to the ground; blood and guts seeped out of its tiny orifices.

"Let's get out of here," said Darryl, looking with panic at his friend, who was clutching his injury. He grabbed the edge of the hole and hoisted himself up. Turning around, he gave Clyde a lift back up onto level ground.

"What the hell was that?!" asked Clyde as they made their way back to the truck. "Do you think it had rabies or something?"

"Must have been," said Darryl, looking at Clyde's raw, red cheek. "No healthy squirrel would charge at a man like that. You'll need to get a shot at the hospital, real quick. I hope that idiot kid didn't drive off with the truck."

They were about twenty yards from the vehicle when another set of red eyes appeared in front of them. Then another. Suddenly, twelve glowing eyes shone back at them like a string of Christmas lights.

Darryl took another step toward the vehicle and a set of glowing, red eyes ran along the ground and leapt at his legs. The squirrel's teeth dug into his shin, piercing through his jeans and skin like a steak knife through cheesecloth.

76

Clyde watched in horror as another squirrel charged at Darryl and attached itself to his other leg. The way it darted toward him it was as if the rodent were guided by some unseen force.

He ran over to Darryl and kicked the squirrels away. But two more came charging not a second later. He could see the rest of them moving forward, poised to attack.

Darryl and Clyde ran away as fast as they could, a pack of red eyes trailing behind them by just a few yards. Their truck blocked, they made for Parker's office near the western gate of the cemetery.

More and more eyes lit up around them as they ran through the dark. And they weren't just squirrels either. There were deer, raccoons, rabbits. Darryl could have sworn he even saw some *frogs* with the evil eyes in the cemetery chapel's reflecting pond.

They reached Parker's office and banged on the door, hooting and hollering for help. A water bowl with a sign labeled HOOCH was set on the stoop next to a chewed-up bone.

"Parker! Let us in!" screamed Clyde as he beat his fist on the hard, pine door.

"What the hell do you two want?" said Parker, muffled, from behind the door.

"The animals in the cemetery. They're possessed or something," said Darryl. "I know it sounds crazy, but they bit Clyde's face and attacked me, too. You gotta let us in."

Parker swung the door open. "Are you guys drunk? What the hell are you talking about?" He was about to give them a good talking to—but stopped when he saw what was behind them.

The creatures of the forest, the vermin, were moving toward them, squealing, their eyes ruby red, teeth and horns bared. It was like he had opened the door to a nightmare.

"What the fuck!" Parker quickly slammed the door shut, leaving Darryl and Clyde outside, the beasts just yards away.

"Parker! You bastard!" yelled Darryl, pulling on the doorknob, to no avail.

A few seconds later they heard Parker scream, but it wasn't in anger. Clyde and Darryl looked through his office window to see Hooch, red-eyed and possessed by an incomprehensible rage. The dog was on top of him, tearing his arm open.

The door swung open again a few seconds later and Parker came out screaming, Hooch chasing right behind him. Parker made it no more than ten yards when the dog knocked him down to the ground.

Parker screamed at Hooch— "Heel! Sit, boy!" —but it was no use. The dog came down on him and tore open his throat. Blood gushed out like water in a fire hydrant. A pack of squirrels jumped out of a nearby tree and rushed over to feed on the rest of him.

With the beasts distracted by their supper, Clyde and Darryl booked it toward the truck. On their way back, they saw more eyes come out from behind trees and graves and move in their direction. They arrived at the truck and Clyde practically dove through the window. Darryl paused in horror, recognizing the half-eaten corpse of his cousin Seth slouched against the passenger side door.

"You drive," said Darryl. "I'll deal with these critters." He hopped into the back of the truck, grabbed a spare shovel, and took an attack position as he wrapped his arm around a loose leather strap.

"What the hell are you doing?!" Clyde exclaimed as he fired up the truck and hit the accelerator.

"These c'yotes killed my cousin!"

"Well, hold on then!" Clyde turned the truck back onto the gravel path as a pack of coyotes emerged from the tree line of Valleyview Forest.

One of them, a larger specimen, jumped toward Darryl. He swung and connected with the predator, sending it to the ground, where it was trampled by others in the pack. Three other coyotes followed and Darryl played home run derby with them, whacking them this way and that.

The truck was nearing the east gate of the cemetery when two more coyotes, bigger and meaner than the ones before, jumped up on the bed. One of them had a piece of a familiar redhead's scalp dangling from its teeth. It made Darryl nearly puke in rage.

He swung and connected with it, sending it off the side of the truck, but the other one bit his leg. He fell down on the bed as the leather strap broke from the bed. He screamed in agony. The creature released his leg and jump on top of him, its teeth inches away. He could feel its warm breath on his face as he pushed the shaft of the shovel against the coyote's neck. Up close, its eyes looked aflame.

Clyde looked back and shouted, "Darryl, hold on tight!"

Darryl grabbed the side of the truck and Clyde pulled a sharp and sudden turn. The truck tilted on its side until it was practically on two wheels, sending the coyote off the bed.

They heard a loud *thunk* as the truck ran over the creature's body.

Clyde pushed the pedal to the floor and sped toward the gate. There was a loud *smash* as the front bumper drove the gate off its hinges and sent it crashing onto the sidewalk. The gravediggers (who would never dig another grave again) sped off into the night.

Dawn approached. Two by two, the red eyes of the cemetery faded into the early morning light.

Dead Can Dance

"Riddle House" by post-punk band The Birthday Party blared in Eric Verlaine's headphones as he approached his maroon locker at Lestershire High. He kept his Walkman cranked to the max at all times; that way he didn't have to hear their taunts.

Eric was dressed head to toe in black—a Damned T-shirt, pegged pants, and a leather jacket with pins of all his favorite death-rock bands. He stood in sharp contrast to his pastel-garbed classmates. Even the New Wavers with their neons and checkerboard looked normal in comparison.

He opened his locker and stuffed some textbooks inside. He grabbed a book of Rimbaud poems from the top shelf and was about to shut the door when Blane Easton, Dave Standish, and Kevin Ryerson—three of 'Shire High's worst—walked up and pinned him against his locker.

"Hey, faggot," said Blane, the de facto leader of the squad. He wore a white cardigan and boat shoes, and all the frizzy-haired girls wanted a piece of him. "I didn't know it was Halloween already."

Kevin, who had the IQ of a rock, and a face to match, chimed in. "Yeah," he snorted. "What do you think you're doing, Verlaine, going trick-or-treating or something?"

Dave didn't say anything. He just stared at Eric and smirked; it was almost worse.

"What's your guys' problem?" asked Eric. "What the hell did I do to you?"

Blane smacked the book of poems out of Eric's hand. "Nothing. We just don't like spooky homos. It's as simple as that."

A small crowd had gathered around the locker, wondering what the popular kids were going to do to the weird goth. Kyle Lucas, a junior, whispered to some of his classmates that Eric liked to take cats to Valleyview Cemetery and skin them and squeeze their blood out into a jar that he kept in his bedroom. Kyle had never seen Eric outside of school, but the whole thing sure sounded believable to his classmates.

Eric leaned down to pick up his book, but Kevin put his big, grimy sneaker down on his knuckle. He cried out in pain as he felt the full weight of the star linebacker on his hand.

The three laughed as tears ran down Eric's cheeks. When they had gotten their fill, they walked down the hall—but not before Blane called out "We'll see you tomorrow, Dracula."

Eric picked up his book and brushed it off. He looked up to see a group of his classmates staring at him bug-eyed, like he was some sort of sideshow act. *Step right up and feast your eyes on the terrible, horrible Teenage Goth!*

The school bell rang at 3 p.m. and Eric escaped the confines of Lestershire High. He walked to the north side of town to hang out with his friends, who were waiting for him in the cemetery. They were *always* there for him.

Jonathan Trumbell. Mira Parker. Abraham Hill. Sabrina Snow. They had all died more than a century ago, but they intrigued Eric. They once had loves and hates and passions just like him, he thought. When he lay down in the cemetery grass among their graves, he felt at peace—as if he and the deceased were on the same plane.

"Hi, guys," he said as he approached the crop of graves tucked away in a far corner of the cemetery. He didn't know a thing about them. But he imagined them as former poets, artists, great thinkers of a bygone era. Before the likes of Duran Duran.

Before heading home, he pulled out a book of his poems and started to read aloud something he had recently wrote.

82

"Tell me of your totem stones,
of the spaces I can't know,
of the life of your body
before your bones
had turned from the gristle,
when I'd only been a blade of grass
'tween your thumbs while you whistled"

*   *   *

Mr. Sanzo, the gym teacher, blew his whistle and the kids in fourth-period gym class started their mandatory jumping-jack/push-up routine.

Eric was at the far end of the gym, dressed in a black tank top, running shorts, and a pair of beat-up Chuck Taylors. He was going through the motions, wishing he were off in some quiet place, preferably the cemetery, free to focus on his art. Maybe write a few blank stanzas on the monotonous day to day of the American teenager. But no, he was stuck in some sweaty, smelly gym in the fucking 1980s.

Blane and Dave were there as well, and they were impossible to ignore. They stared at him and made gestures he wouldn't repeat to his stepfather on his worst day. When he looked back at them they laughed and high-fived each other. He wished he could curl up into a ball underneath the bleachers.

Mr. Sanzo broke everyone off into groups and had them do lay-up drills. As luck would have it, Eric was placed in the same group as Blane. He was standing at center court, waiting for the guy in front of him to pass him the basketball, when he felt a draft on his backside and saw his shorts (and tightie-whities) pulled down to his sneakers.

83

He turned around to see his classmates pointing and laughing at his pale, bare ass. Blane stood directly behind him, a devious smile on his face. Eric quickly pulled up his shorts and charged at him. He landed one weak punch to his shoulder and Blane retaliated with a swift jab to his gut. Before Eric could land another punch, Mr. Sanzo rushed over and got between the two.

"Verlaine, what the hell do you think you're doing?!" yelled Mr. Sanzo.

"But Mr. Sanzo, Blane pulled down my shorts and..."

"I don't want to hear who started what, alright? Come with me."

Blane leered at Eric and mouthed the word 'faggot' as Mr. Sanzo led them out of the gym and toward Principal Coscarelli's office.

"Were people so screwed up when you were alive?" asked Eric, as he looked down, red-faced and teary-eyed, at the grave of Jonathan Trumbell. "I think I live in the Age of Idiocy." Mr. Trumbell had died more than 100 years prior, but he was as real and alive to Eric as anybody in his daily life. Probably more so.

"Everybody thinks I'm some freak. It's like Oscar Wilde. The Victorians vilified him for not sticking to the status quo. I know I'm no Oscar Wilde, but it's the same shit, different century."

The wind blew through the nearby trees, and Eric could have sworn he heard a whisper.

Eric was drinking from the water fountain outside of biology class the following day when Helen Tierney walked up to him and said hello. He turned around and wiped some excess water from his chin. He wasn't used to people greeting him in the hallway, not unless they were there to torment him.

84

Helen wasn't one of the popular girls, but she we no outcast either; she kind of skirted the line between punk and straight. She liked the Go-Go's and went to punk shows, but she was friends with girls on the cheerleading squad and her dad owned a baseball card shop down on Memorial Drive. She was pretty in an old-fashioned kind of way and wore funky looking dresses.

"Hi, Helen," said Eric, nervously.

Helen smiled at him. "Nice shirt."

He looked down. Morrissey and the rest of The Smiths were printed on the front, standing on some bleak English street, looking cool as shit. "Thanks."

"Hey, there's a party at Claire Ziering's house tonight. Should be a blast. You should come hang with me and my friends."

Eric hadn't been to a party since his friend's *Empire Strikes Back*-themed shindig in middle school. And there were no *girls* at that one.

"I'm not really sure if I can come," said Eric. "I kind of have to..."

"It will be fun," said Helen, sensing his unease. She sweetened the proposition. "Going to be plenty of good music: The Cult, Oingo Boingo, Boomtown Rats. What do you say?"

"Sure," he said, a tiny smile cracking through his morose exterior. "What time should I show up?"

Claire Ziering's luxurious house sat on a sharp hill overlooking the town of Lestershire. It was only a short drive from the cemetery and the town's business district. The close proximity to Valleyview and his ancient friends made Eric feel a little less uneasy as he entered Claire's house.

Her parents were on vacation in Cabo, so the party was an all-out blitz. One hundred or so students from 'Shire High were crammed in the various rooms of the house. "Shout" by Tears for Fears was blasting through the Ziering's top-of-the-line Sony stereo. Empty Miller Lite cans littered the floor.

"Eric, over here," Helen called from the kitchen. She was standing with some of her friends Eric recognized from school. Much to his surprise, they all waved and smiled at him.

The next hour was something akin to a dream. Helen's friends were as nice as can be. They laughed, made fun of some of 'Shire High's worst teachers and talked pop culture. They all marveled at Eric's encyclopedic knowledge of music and literature. For the first time in years, he felt accepted. He wondered, *could I actually make some living, breathing friends?*

The fun was interrupted by the sound of Blane screaming from the front door. "Are you fucking kidding me?! Eric Verlaine? Who the hell let this queer in?" Kevin and Dave stood behind him like silent guards.

Eric's chest felt tight. Everyone in the party was staring at him. It was like the hallway at school all over again.

"We did," said Helen, defiantly. She scowled at Blane and nodded back toward her friends. "You got a problem with that?"

"Tierney, you're too good for this creep," said Blane. "Since when did you start associating with the scum of the valley?"

Maybe it was the alcohol. Or maybe he just couldn't stand there and let this *dick* attack his newfound friend. Eric walked out into the living room and got face-to-face with Blane.

Blane laughed. "What do you think you're doing, Verlaine? You want to *kiss* me or something...*faggot?*"

A rage fueled by months of torment reached a breaking point and Eric charged at Blane like a bull. He knocked him into a coffee table, sending an expensive lamp crashing to the floor. Kevin and Dave quickly pulled him off Blane and started pummeling him.

"Get off him!" said Charles Beaumont, a junior on the cross-country team. He and another one of Helen's friends pushed Blane's goons away, giving Eric enough room to run out the front door.

Eric dashed down Claire's driveway and kept running. His house was two miles away, and it was getting late, so he headed to the only place he felt safe: Valleyview Cemetery. When he got to his favorite spot, he stopped to catch his breath. The graves of his friends looked different under the light of the moon, though no less welcoming.

Eric told them about the party and what happened, about how amazing it felt to talk to kids his age, and how shitty Blane and his buddies were. "That kid deserves a beating," he said, looking down at Abraham Hill's grave.

That's when he heard a voice.

"Who the hell are you talking to, *faggot*?"

It was Blane. Kevin and Dave were standing there, too. They were drunk, and angry.

"Go away, Blane!" shouted Eric. "You're not welcome here!"

"That's it, you creepy fuck. You're dead."

Blane ran up to Eric and clobbered him in the face, sending him down to the cold cemetery grass. Before Eric had a chance to recover, Kevin and Dave started kicking him in the ribs.

Eric screamed out in agony. "Help me! Help!"

Blane grabbed him by his leather jacket and pulled him up from the ground. "No one is going to help you. You chose the wrong place to hide."

He pushed Eric toward Kevin, who socked him in the stomach. Eric cried out in pain as Kevin pushed him toward Dave, who kicked him in the nuts and elbowed him in the face.

The three of them passed Eric around like a doll—back and forth, back and forth. Blood streamed down his bruised, swollen face. He was a small kid, and they had no idea how close to death they were driving him.

Finally, they dropped him to the ground and stood in front of him, laughing.

Behind their backs, Eric saw movement out of the corner of his throbbing eye. Four transparent shapes were rising from the ground. They had a dayglo green shade to them, like the black light posters hanging in his bedroom. They ranged in height from about 5 feet to a little over 6, and they seemed to be dressed in the clothing of a bygone era.

They drew closer to his attackers, and that's when it hit him—these were his friends, his dead friends. They took on more of a corporeal shape, and he could make out individual features of each entity. One of the guys looked like the frontman for some New Romantic band like Spandau Ballet. But *that* guy didn't have flesh hanging from his face like this one. Eric wondered, in awe of the moment, *Is that Abraham or Jonathan?*

Suddenly Blane, Kevin, and Dave were whisked into the air, ten feet up. They screamed as they looked down and saw the ravenous, glowing bodies hoisting them up. The ghosts dropped Blane and his lackeys, and they screamed as they connected with the ground.

The attack continued for several minutes. Blane was thrown headfirst into an obelisk. Kevin was kicked back against a marble angel. Dave's mouth was stuffed full of dirt and worms and godknowswhat. Finally, after a few broken bones and a half a pint of blood, the ghosts let them go. They ran screaming out of the cemetery and towards Blane's BMW.

Eric watched as Blane's car sped away wildly. He turned to the ghosts and smiled. "Thank you."

They looked at him and nodded, before drifting downward and disappearing into the dirt.

About thirty seconds later, Eric heard a loud crash up the road and saw a large flame shoot up into the sky.

*   *   *

The loudspeaker in the hallway clicked and out drifted the muffled voice of Lestershire High's principal. "I'm sure you're all aware of the accident that took the lives of Blane Easton, Dave Standish, and Kevin Ryerson this past weekend. A counselor is standing by for those impacted by this event. May this serve as a tragic reminder that you should never drink and drive."

The announcement ended and Eric and his new friends continued their conversation. Eric's face was still pretty banged up from the other night.

"Can't believe what happened to those guys," said Helen to Eric and her other friends. "They were assholes, but geez."

Eric thought about the ghosts. He saw the faces of Blane, Dave, and Kevin screaming, a look of manic terror in their eyes as the avenging spirits clawed at them and threw them around like cats toying with mice.

The group discussed their deceased classmates for a couple minutes more before the bell rang.

"So we'll see you at the arcade later?" said Helen.

"Definitely," said Eric. He waved goodbye to his new friends and shut his locker.

He walked down the hallway, clad in black, holding his poems. And no one bothered him.

See Appendix C *for more of Eric's morbid poetry.*

Easy Prey

He first noticed the well-to-do, thirtysomething couple walking their terrier from his seat at the Broadview Diner lunch counter. It was a great observation point for looking out across the western portion of the cemetery. Normally, there wasn't much to watch—it was more like a meditation—and the man at the diner, whom the regulars knew as 'Tommy,' had plenty of time to think. Soon enough, Tommy was scheduling his Saturday evening dinners around the couple's little trek—watching and waiting.

The woman looked good—prim, black walking heels, bundled up in an expensive fur-fringed jacket. The guy on her arm was a little more disheveled, but he wore nice clothes and had a fat, expensive-looking watch on his wrist. Tommy never saw them go in or out of the cemetery, and the pair certainly never stopped by his favored slop house.

They walked the semi-circle at the same time and stopped at the same grave each week. The man at the counter was timing them, irritated that he never saw the pair enter or exit the west gate. They would pause at the grave for about ten minutes, the dog would sit patiently at the woman's feet, then Tommy would lose sight of them behind stones, shrubbery, and trees as they continued on the other half of the path.

It seemed like there was always some disruption that prevented Tommy from tracking their coming and going. One week it was this melted-cheese blob of a couple blocking the window as they struggled to remove their coats and get situated for their slovenly feast. Another time it was the plain-faced, track-marked waitress trying to chat him up that drew his attention away during those crucial minutes just before 8 p.m.

Tommy didn't get mad at the waitress or the other working class folk he shared most of his meals with. The diner people were his kind of people. He knew more than a few of the regulars had done a stretch or two. He sat there at that counter staring out the window, thinking about the couple who walked the dog.

He eventually dreamed up a whole story for them—the wealthy couple with their palace in the hills above the cemetery slope, how they spent their money on extravagant things while he moldered away in the valley. Just thinking about it pissed him off.

He wouldn't mind spending some of their money—snatch a credit or ATM card, a checkbook, a few hundred in cash, and spend a night at the nice motel just up the road, as opposed to the hovels he had been drifting in and out of since parole.

There was something about the woman that got him all worked up. The way she carried herself just maddeningly turned him on, while also simultaneously enraging him over his own lot in life. Tommy grew jealous of her pathetic-looking husband. He knew that eventually his idle jealousy would lead him to act, but he had to make sure he wouldn't get caught and sent back to County.

It was finally the Saturday night that Tommy's plans would come to fruition. All those weeks he sat studying and timing the couple would soon pay off. He went into the graveyard twenty minutes before their usual time and waited. It was 7:55, and maybe five degrees, with a nipping breeze, when he crouched just out of sight of the grave they regularly approached. He had taken the time and made sure no eyes had followed him in. A light snow shower aided his stealth.

Tommy heard the dog first. A little pitter-patter on the pavement, slight panting breaths. He didn't make a sound as he fingered the outline of his knife over his pants pocket.

When he thought they'd passed out of sight of the diner window, he jumped out of his hiding spot, grabbing a handful of the woman's jacket. Tommy was surprised at how easily she slipped out of her coat and soundlessly ran off between a row of mausoleums.

Her husband lunged at him, but Tommy had his knife ready and drove it into the guy's chest. He was a weak man and fell to the ground, grasping at his injury, making very little sound. Tommy figured he must have hit a lung, as the man couldn't scream for help.

Tommy was astonished at how hard the little dog bit down on his thumb and forefinger. He nearly dropped the knife. But he was able to throw the canine against a particularly large marble headstone, where it let out a sharp yelp.

Once two of the three were dealt with, he went after the woman, his heart pounding in his throat. He hated running, and when he caught her he was going to do more than take her purse...

*   *   *

Early the next morning, as he drank his coffee in his shack, the cemetery's caretaker calmly contacted the police about the body in the snow. He had seen this sort of thing before and hoped the ambulance would arrive soon and move the corpse, as it was in view of his favorite breakfast spot.

There had been a stabbing in the cemetery overnight. He had seen the wealthy guy around, from time to time, visiting his wife's grave. He had been the one that found the unconscious victim on the path and drove him to the ER. There was something about that small section near the western gate (within full view of the Broadview) that drew in the crazies, addicts, and the general bottom-feeders in town.

When the police arrived, they found 'Tommy' with a woman's fur-fringed jacket in hand, not thirty feet from where the caretaker claimed he'd found the stabbing victim. The mugger's face was frozen in a ghastly agony, corpse-white, and he had large red stains and bits and pieces of dangling, mutilated flesh concentrated around his crotch area. They noted the little dog's tracks in the snow and Tommy's wild path through the cemetery, which seemed to go in circles.

After a brief questioning, the police told the caretaker that the man he brought in to the hospital would likely be fine, and that he had probably saved his life. The caretaker told the officers that he couldn't take credit for saving the man, that it was blind luck that he'd spotted the wandering terrier when he did, and drove his truck over to investigate.

The coroner's report, regarding the perpetrator found dead in Valleyview Cemetery, didn't go into detail beyond the toxicology readings (which came back clean), but she did comment that the wounding to the penis and testes was certainly not the primary cause of death—which was recorded as 'exhaustion/extreme dehydration.'

Randall's Complex

January 16

It being the 16th of the month, Randall Orr left his data entry job at Fleishman Associates, bought a bouquet of mums from Allen Flowers, and went to Valleyview Cemetery to visit his mother.

Rebecca Orr had passed away on May 16, 1992. At the time of his mother's death, Randall was still living with her. The pair had been attached at the hip since the severing of the umbilicus, and his lack of a career or a long-term relationship proved it. The adult world was just too much for him. So when she keeled over on that cool spring day from sudden cardiac arrest, he had no one and nothing to turn to.

The 16th was his day with Mom. He couldn't go with her to the flea market or Phil's Steak House like he used to, but he could drop by with some of her favorite flowers and have a heart-to-heart. There was just one problem; Valleyview Cemetery, Mrs. Orr's eternal resting place, scared the living daylights out of him. She was buried under an oak tree in a far corner of the cemetery, just a stone's throw from the back fence.

During the winter month, by the time Randall got out of work, bought her flowers, and made his way across town, the sun was already setting, and that patch of dirt that contained his dear mother was already partially shrouded in darkness. He always made sure to leave her grave before the entire place fell into shadow; that would have sent him over the edge. No matter how terrified he was, however, he couldn't miss his monthly visit.

It was 4:30 when he walked up to her grave and placed the bouquet of flowers delicately against her headstone. "Hi, mom," he said, as he knelt down in front of her grave. "It's me again."

He stopped and stared at the grave, as if waiting to hear her raspy voice talk back. "I sure miss ya," he said. He paused and tried to think of something interesting to say, but it had been a pretty slow month.

As usual, he informed her of all of the near-death and potentially cataclysmic things that had occurred to him over the past 30 days. There was the car that took the same four turns behind him on his way home from work the previous week. He had avoided that *madman* by pulling into a driveway, turning off his lights, and waiting ten minutes.

Then there was the cheese. He bought a block of Crowley's sharp cheddar cheese from Akel Markets and had eaten a few pieces before noticing it was moldy. To avoid potential poisoning, he underwent an intense herbal cleanse (i.e. he guzzled vinegar for three days.)

This went on for half an hour, his sharing of the full, dull details of his paranoid existence to the indifferent corpse below. He looked at his watch. *4:52.* He'd gone on a little longer than usual, and a shuddering gloom crept over the cemetery.

"Mom, I'm sorry, but I've got to go. It's getting on, and you know how I feel about being out this late. I love you, and I'll see you next month." He hurried out of the cemetery as the sun hit the edge of the horizon, its golden rays replaced by the unmerciful blackness of night.

February 16

Randall pushed the pedal to the floor of his '88 Buick LeSabre and slammed his fist on the steering wheel. "C'mon, c'mon!" he said, as he waited for the light to change at an intersection. The flowers from Allen's lay on the passenger seat, thrown there haphazardly as he had rushed into the car.

His last meeting at work had run extra-long, and he hadn't been able to leave the office until 4:30. To make matters worse, he had to stand in line at Allen's while a customer reamed the owner out for not delivering flowers to his wife on Valentine's Day. He nearly had a panic attack in witnessing the altercation.

When he walked in, the guy was leaning over the counter, his hands pressed hard into the wood, like he was about to jump the florist. Randall rehearsed all of the probable outcomes of the confrontation. *The owner's not going to give him what he wants and he's going to get mad and they're going to yell at each other back and forth until the guy pulls out a gun and shoots the owner, and since I'm a witness he'll probably shoot me, too. Or maybe he'll see me looking at him funny and kick my ass, slam my head into the cooler, and drop a vase on me. I don't know who this guy is. He could be a mob boss or drug dealer for all I know. Oh, my god.*

Luckily for Randall, he left the scene unscathed. The owner gave the customer a refund and he left smiling. *But it could have gone badly,* thought Randall. *You have to be prepared for every contingency.*

He parked in front of the cemetery and hurried to the gate. He had never entered this late before. It was *too* dark. Every ounce of his being told him he should turn around, that only doom and terror awaited him if he went in. But the calmer side that he popped 100mg of Zoloft a day to maintain made him move onward.

I'll make it really quick, he told himself as he neared his mother's little corner of the cemetery. *Just a "hi, how are you, I got to go" sort of thing. That will be good enough for this month. Mom will have to understand.*

He approached her grave and set the flowers down. He had never seen her headstone look so dreary, so gray. A small sliver of light cut across the family name, ORR in big, blocky letters. All he could hear was his own breath and the brisk wind blowing through the trees.

"Hi mom," he said, more nervous than usual. "I'm sorry I'm so late." He explained his workplace predicament and the incident at the flower shop to his mother, all the while watching the sky darken. He didn't think it was possible for light to recede so quickly.

He looked at his watch. It was 4:52. He knew the cemetery hours like the back of his hand; the caretaker closed the front gate at 5 p.m. sharp in winter.

"Mom, I gotta go," he said, the words slipping out through stuttered breaths. "I'll see you next month, okay? Bye!"

He ran, up and over a hill teeming with mausoleums. His mother's grave was located ten or so yards from the back fence, and he had underestimated how hard it would be to navigate back to the front gate in the dark. His feet pounded on the gravel path, scattering little pebbles, sending a loud *crunch-crunch-crunch* through the cemetery. Sweat dripped down his face and stung as it hit the February freeze.

He looked down at this watch. It was 4:55. He still had time.

But when he turned the corner onto the main path out of the cemetery, his heart sank. The large, iron gate was closed, its eight-foot posts towering over him. A heavy-duty steel lock hung from the bars.

No no no no. This can't be. It's not 5 yet.

He looked at his watch again. It still said 4:55—but the second hand wasn't moving. He wasn't sure when the watch had frozen, but it was certainly well past 5 p.m.; the moon was high in the sky, casting a bright, white light on his worried face.

He tugged at the lock, hoping it was old and worn and would break off, but it was solid. *It would take a good set of wire cutters to break that sucker off.* He thought about climbing up and over the fence, but the entire cemetery was surrounded

98

by spear-like iron posts, the kind you would see around a castle in some schlocky horror flick.

Terrible thoughts started to flood his brain, as if the levee holding back all of his worries had suddenly exploded. He was used to seeing the absolute worst in any situation, but this was a new dimension of terror.

That's when he saw it.

At first, he thought it a shadow. Maybe a car passing by down the street, throwing the light off. But there were no cars around; not a single one had passed by in the last ten minutes. Besides, shadows don't *move* like that.

Randall couldn't pinpoint what he was looking at. There was no analog, nothing that existed in nature to compare it to. It resembled a human being only superficially; it had two arms, two legs, and something akin to a head. It's "skin" was black and oily, and as the thing moved, its outer layer slid around like some kind of sludge, making a sickening squeezing noise with each "step" forward. And despite its loose, dripping appearance, it was moving fast—in Randall's direction.

He juked between trees and mausoleums, running as fast as he could from the creature. Sitting in an office chair for eight hours a day had sapped most of his fitness over the years, but the sight of the creature's gelatinous, bog-like body added a much-needed spring to his step. He turned around and saw it slide over a tombstone. What looked like its torso plopped down on the frozen dirt and sprung back up, as if the laws of physics had ceased to exist.

Randall knew he couldn't keep this game up all night. The gates were locked, and eventually this thing would gain on him. He thought of its slimy, tar-like flesh, enveloping his body, sucking up his bones and organs like a Hoover from hell.

He was yards from his mother's grave when he got an idea. Her tombstone was several feet away from a mausoleum, which itself was just yards from the cemetery fence. If he could hop from her tombstone onto the mausoleum, he could leap over the fence and out of this nightmare.

The creature was just yards behind, its incomprehensible form sloshing toward him. He readied himself for the leap, throwing his elbows out to his side and ducking, as the creature's extremities reached out toward him, its shapeless hands mere inches from his body.

He leapt on top of his mother's tombstone as the creature's black fingers came down, barely missing him. The gap between the tombstone and mausoleum was longer than he estimated, but he used his momentum to fling himself onto the stone roof. He looked at the cemetery fence. It was a relatively long jump. He steadied himself to get a running start.

Just then the creature's slimy hand grabbed his ankle and started to pull. He kicked at it and broke free, but the creature's rubbery appendage extended and reached toward him again. Randall looked back and saw its face, a horrific assemblage of teeth, bone, and boils. It leered at him with unfathomable glee, as if he had been waiting for him in the cemetery since the dawn of time.

Giving it all his sad and worn-out body could, Randall rushed from the mausoleum and leapt into the night sky.

*   *   *

Chief Burnett stepped out of his squad car with his morning coffee and walked over to the cemetery fence, where the coroner and several of his officers were already gathered. Forrester, the newest guy on the force, turned away and puked.

"Christ, Forrester," said Burnett. "You nearly spewed on my new shoes."

When Burnett saw the body impaled on the fence, he too nearly emptied his stomach.

Randall Orr was hanging there like some half-assed scarecrow, slumped over, a sharp, blood-soaked spike sticking out from his chest. He had a deranged look on his face, which had grown white from the loss of blood and the February freeze.

"Goddamn junkies," said Burnett to the coroner, who was getting ready for Forrester and the other unlucky rookies to lift Randall's body off the post and onto a stretcher. "This guy must have been on PCP. Who the *fuck* would try jumping that?"

Moira's Homecoming

Richie and his new wife, Moira, were just married and expecting a baby. After a short honeymoon in the Finger Lakes, they were driving to Moira's hometown of Lestershire. Her mother, Edith, was a midwife and they wanted her to deliver the child.

"Richie, before we get to my mom's, I want to introduce you to my daddy," said Moira, who sat in the passenger seat, rubbing her belly.

Richie and Moira had met the previous fall as students at the university, which sat just across the river from Lestershire. He was a grad student and she was a sophomore. Despite the proximity, Richie had never stepped foot in Lestershire.

They crossed the river and drove into town. Little mom-and-pop shops dotted the thoroughfare, a sharp contrast to the abandoned storefronts Richie had grown accustomed to seeing upstate.

"Turn left at this light and pull into the parking area before the chapel," said Moira. "We'll get out and walk up."

Richie parked and helped Moira out of her seat. She had a little trouble getting the seatbelt off over her swollen belly. He held her by the arm and helped her traverse the gravel path that led to her father's grave.

"So we're looking for a mausoleum, right?" said Richie.

Moira hesitated before shaking her head. "No, we moved him from the mausoleum...and buried him."

The way she hesitated made Richie recall what happened at the county clerk's office the week before, while applying for their marriage certificate. Moira wasn't 22 as she said she was; she was 24 and actually a year older than him.

They exchanged terse words; things got so heated that the clerk had to ask them to keep it down.

They walked further into the cemetery and Moira paused. She wobbled and told Richie she felt lightheaded and wanted to go back to the car.

Richie sighed. "Moira, why didn't we just *drive* up here?

Moira broke into tears and Richie walked her back to the car, chalking her behavior up to a late-pregnancy, hormone-induced mood swing. They drove out of the cemetery and made their way across town to Edith's house.

Moira hadn't stretched the truth when she had told Richie that she hadn't come from money. The house was dilapidated. It seemed to sink into the ground, as if something was pulling at it from below. Tall weeds sprouted from the earth and the side yard served as the final resting place for a number of rusted-out automobiles.

When they walked up the front steps Richie half-expected some old crone with a pointy black hat to come out, cackling. Instead, out walked a woman with Moira's hazel eyes and welcoming smile, albeit a decade older than he had expected. She went to Moira first and gave her a big hug, before rubbing her daughter's belly and whispering to her grandchild-to-be.

"And you must be Richie," said Edith. She gave him a fierce hug. "It's so nice to meet you. We have *big* plans for you and our daughter."

Richie and Moira followed Edith inside and sat down for a lunch of roast beef and potatoes. Richie kept his eyes focused on the plate so as to avoid looking at the yellowed, peeling wallpaper and the mound of dead flies piled up in the overhead light.

"I still can't believe my daughter is going to be the first Clegg to graduate from college," said Edith. "Just two more semesters, right dear?"

Richie looked up from his plate and swallowed a mouthful of potato. "*Two* more semesters?" He looked at the women quizzically; he knew Moira was nowhere near completing her degree, but his query went unanswered.

"I'm so happy to have my Moira back home. It's been so long. I can't wait for all three of you to live here with Sybil and me. Oh, it will be wonderful."

Richie stopped chewing and looked at his wife in a way that said he was more than irritated.

"You two finish up and I'll go wash the dishes," said Edith. She went into the kitchen, leaving Richie and Moira alone.

"What the hell is your mother talking about? Does she actually think we're going to live *here*?" asked Richie, with a hint of disgust at the prospect. Moira looked like she was on the verge of tears and wouldn't make eye contact with her husband.

Richie, having had enough of her lies and half-truths for the day, got up and left.

"Richie, wait!" But he was already out the door and backing out of the driveway.

He gripped the steering wheel tightly and sped away from the house, not sure where he was headed. His parents lived four hours away in Vermont and the lease on his apartment had ended at the beginning of the summer. He and Moira talked about finding a place near the university, and he had applications out at a few of the local private schools in need of English tutors.

Realizing he couldn't just drive aimlessly for hours (and that he had been barely able to swallow food in that nasty excuse for a dining room), Richie stopped at the Broadview Diner, just past the cemetery.

He found a seat at the counter and sat down, fuming.

Move in? Move in?! What do I really know about this girl? And we're having a kid... She told me she was on birth control—

and *I was protected. I'm 23 and haven't finished my master's—I make next to nothing as a TA...*

"Can I help you, sir?" said the cook behind the counter.

"Not unless you've got scotch back there." Richie gave a halfhearted grin.

The cook laughed and handed him a menu. "I wish. What's the matter, fella? Woman trouble?"

"Yeah, my wife Moira is driving me—" He paused at the cook's seeming recognition of the name. He figured in a small town he wouldn't want to accidentally badmouth someone's cousin or niece.

"I know Moira. My name's Al. So *you're* Richie?"

Richie was taken aback and wasn't sure how to proceed. Al smiled at him and continued. "I've known her since she was a little kid. A real sweet girl, close to her family. Lucky guy."

Richie relaxed. "We probably should've gotten to know each other better before we rushed into this."

"No woman is going to tell you everything up front, buddy. That's just the way they are." Al smirked at Richie.

"Outright lies, though?"

"The point is, they don't consider themselves liars and want to present to you the best version of themselves. And they usually have the best of intentions too, that's the thing. So, you can either go out and try to find the ultimate, unabashed truth of things—or you can do what the rest of us do and let them live out their little fantasies."

Richie half-smiled, not exactly consoled about the matter or by the older man's dated outlook on women. He finished his burger with his thoughts and decided it would be best to head back to his wife and unborn child.

He returned to Edith's place and immediately apologized to both his mother-in-law and Moira for leaving so suddenly. Moira didn't push him, and they went to bed as a functioning married couple.

The next morning, they attended a memorial for Moira's father at the cemetery. When they arrived, Moira's aunt Sybil was standing at her father's grave with two unfamiliar men.

As they approached, Richie could hear the group chanting, partaking in some sort of strange ritual. Moira pointed out Jerry and Carl to Richie, but the group made no notice of the coming couple. The whole thing made Richie feel uncomfortable and out of place.

The grave itself was just a flat granite marker inscribed with the name 'CLEGG'. He felt sorry that Moira thought she had to lie about her own father's final resting place. When he turned to her, she was chanting along with them, almost in a trance. Her face seemed vacant of her normal, vibrant range of expression. The speech was unfamiliar to him.

Richie was a Renaissance scholar with a specialty in Romantic literature. He was well-acquainted with most Latin-based languages, and quite a few of the Slavonic ones—so to hear something so foreign that he couldn't make out any of the words was a curiosity.

When the chanting stopped, the men and women seemed to return to normal. They greeted Moira and Richie briefly before chatting with one another about various events, gossip, and family news. Richie pulled his wife aside and questioned her about what he had just witnessed.

"What was that? I've never heard that language before. Was that a *prayer*?"

Moira looked at her relatives, unsure how to respond. They seemed to be engaged with each other, so she felt at ease to talk quietly with her husband.

"It's an Indian language. Daddy was half-native, but I don't remember which tribe he belonged to. I think we were just asking for the ancestors to return to the land and watch over everybody and keep my father company." Richie nodded at her childish explanation of what was likely a much more complicated ritual.

They were startled from their conversation when her aunt Sybil began arguing vehemently with one of the men that Richie had been briefly introduced to.

"The time is *nigh*, Sybil!" said the man.

"Certainly not. We will wait!" Sybil was in the man's face, her index finger practically jabbing his flabby jowl.

Sybil looked back at Richie and his skin crawled at her intensity. She backed off from the man but continued to berate him in their native language. Edith got involved and was trying to quell her sister's lividity when the other old man stepped in and began arguing with her.

Richie looked to Moira for direction, but she was clutching her belly, overwhelmed by the sudden infighting of her family. He was transfixed as he watched the scene unfold, the intensity and seeming vitriol the men and women spewed at each other over *who knows what.*

When he turned to Moira again, she was gone. He figured it was too much for her, and he jogged back down to the car, expecting to find her crying in the front seat. But when he got to the car, she was nowhere to be seen.

Richie walked the sidewalk in front of the cemetery, looking for his wife, searching the wide expanse of the graveyard to no avail. He could still see her family huddled together around the grave, likely arguing. He went across the street to the deli, hoping she had slipped in for something to drink.

"Good morning, sir. Make sure you see the board for our daily specials," said the butcher as Richie walked in. It was an old Red & White, a small market with a big deli case in the back. He searched the three aisles, then asked the butcher if he had seen a petite redhead walk in.

"Oh yeah, Moira. You must be Richie, then? I saw her walk by not ten minutes ago. Probably headed to her cousin's flower shop just up the block." Richie thanked the man and rushed out of the store. He saw the florist's sign, Allen Flowers, and half-jogged to it.

When he entered the flower shop he was again greeted pleasantly by another one of the town's business folk.

"Hello? What can I do for you?" asked the woman behind the counter.

Richie was now breaking a light sweat, breathing heavier than normal.

"Are you related to Moira Clegg? Have you seen her?" The woman smiled at Richie and asked if she could get him a glass of water. He declined. She came to him from behind the table where she was working on an arrangement. He thought it odd how she felt her way around. When she entered the light from the window Richie could see her eyes were a milky-white, and it made sense. She was blind.

"Hi, Richie. My name is Candy. Moira stopped in for a minute. She was upset about her family, as always."

"Do you know where she went?"

Candy shrugged. "Knowing her, she just needs a few hours to herself. She might have gone to the park for a walk or up into the forest where we used to play as kids."

Richie threw up his hands in frustration.

"She's crazy for you, Richie. She'll find you when she's ready. Go get lunch, visit some shops, and buy her something nice; then come back here and I'll put together a bouquet for you to take to her."

He thanked the woman and walked back down Memorial Drive, noticing Moira's family was gone from the cemetery. He then headed to the now-familiar Broadview Diner.

Richie calmed down as he ate another burger and chatted with Al at the lunch counter. Al was busy with the noontime crowd and didn't have as much advice to offer as he had the night before.

Richie hung around for a few hours, watching the people of Lestershire come and go. His eyes wandered every so often over the cemetery and out onto the street, hoping his wife would appear and they could go home.

He did love Moira. In all honesty, he couldn't deny that he was completely enamored of her when he first saw her wandering through the stacks of the university library. It felt natural to him how soon they became a couple, and how excited they both were when she moved into his apartment.

His parents had taken the news of her pregnancy in stride. Moira and Richie spent many anxiety-filled nights in Vermont at his parents' house planning for the baby's arrival, though both always seemed certain about their future together.

Richie said he was off to find his wife and shook Al's hand.

He wandered the rows of stores, which were beginning to close. There was a women's boutique that looked like it might have some things Moira might like, and he went in. The owner showed him some purses. She too knew Moira.

Richie returned to his car and drove to Edith's house with the new purse he had purchased for Moira. His heart dropped when he discovered no one was home.

He drove around town; it was nearing sundown and he didn't quite know what to do, but he recalled Moira's cousin's offer to make him a special floral arrangement.

When he got to the floral shop it was closed. He sat on the curb out front, thinking. He remembered Candy had said Moira liked to walk the park and the forest. Obviously, the park made more sense for a woman who was expecting to give birth within the month. So he drove down to the nearby park but only found a few kids playing basketball.

"Hey guys, have you seen a pregnant redhead around?" They shook their heads. "Is there a place up on the hill in the woods where people hang out?" Richie asked, pointing toward the forest northeast of the cemetery. The young teens looked at each other, then one of the older kids stepped forward.

"Yeah..." The kid hesitated before continuing, "Just go to the top of Richard Street and keep going." Richie thanked the kid and hurried back to his car. He thought about a depressed, pregnant Moira wandering the forest at dark, and tore up the road from the park.

The street ended at an intersection with another road running east to west. He wasn't quite sure what the kids had meant by 'keep going,' so he parked his car and entered the woods at the T.

It took him a few minutes to find the small trail in the underbrush at dusk, but there was certainly a well-used path to follow into the forest. He walked for ten minutes, passing various campsites, fire pits with broken beer bottles, and ramshackle forts made from plywood.

It was a waste of time. He emerged at the other side of the forest onto a street which led to an elite hilltop neighborhood. He walked down the street, which he assumed, correctly, would lead back to his car. The sun had dipped behind a far hillside, enveloping the river valley in twilight. By now he had far surpassed worry and had entered a full-on panic.

Richie was about to enter his car and head back to Edith's house when he heard Moira scream. It wasn't that he knew her scream—he had just reached the point of despair where the worst possible scenarios made the most sense.

He ran toward the sound, down Richard Street and through residential backyards. The screaming was fairly continuous, almost clockwork with its regularity. He dove into the underbrush and raced through the forest, on a path he assumed would lead to the cemetery.

He saw a faint, flickering light through the trees and ran toward it. The screaming grew louder as he emerged into a semi-clearing. A group of hooded figures in dark robes surrounded the source of light. They parted when they heard him emerge from the bush. That's when he saw her, and he, himself, shrieked at the scene.

Moira was naked, glistening with sweat, splotched with blood, and held down by two hooded figures on a stone slab. Man and wife looked into each other's eyes as they both unleashed terror-ridden howls. Three of the hooded figures held Richie back before he could enter their circle.

"What the hell is going on?! What are you doing to my wife?! Moira!" He was clubbed unconscious from behind.

When he came to, he was lying in an earthen ditch, the hooded figures standing over him. He was drugged and couldn't find words to speak, as the images above flickered in the firelight.

"That's the father?" A man spoke, leaning over the ditch. Richie could make out the man's intense, seemingly demonic features and was instinctually frightened.

Moira appeared by his side, now shrouded in a black robe, beaming as she held their newborn son in her arms.

"Yes, that's my Richie, Daddy." She leaned down. Richie was shocked at the revelation of her father and even more fearful of the unrecognizable, wild look on her face. Other members of the group emerged and looked down into the hole.

"You did it, honey!" Edith was the first he recognized. She stood with her sister; he could see their hands and arms still covered in blood from the delivery.

The two men from the cemetery, one he recalled named Jerry, who had been arguing with Moira's aunt, chuckled when they saw Richie unable to move or speak.

The group began chanting over him, the same ritualistic verse from earlier in the day. More hooded figures appeared, looking down on him. He recognized most of them. Al from the diner. Moira's blind cousin from the floral shop. Nearly everyone he had spoken to that day was there chanting in the unknown native language.

Dirt began raining down on him as they saw to his internment. He screamed in his own head, as no sound could escape his lips. More dirt fell, piling up on his arms, legs, chest, and he felt the weight and the dread of his own horrible burial.

When he could no longer see, and the accumulating mass on his chest suppressed his breathing so much that he thought he was on the verge of passing out, he heard his wife speak her final farewell.

"I love you more than words, Richie. I can't believe we did it! It had to be this way, Richie. Our boy has such an important role—such an important purpose. Someday he will lead my people. We've been waiting for so long to come back home, Richie. You are now a part of something much greater."

One Foot in the Grave

Willie Morris stared out the window of his third-floor room at Floral Nursing and Rehabilitation Center and let out a deep, defeated sigh. His good friend Leonard McDaniel, who lived down the hallway in room 304, had passed from a heart attack the week prior and was now "taking up space," as they called it, across the street at Valleyview Cemetery.

Leonard was a fellow New York Yankees fan, and he and Willie had bonded over their lifelong love for the Bronx Bombers. In fact, upon his death, Leonard left Willie his favorite Yankees cap. Willie kept it in a box in his closet for safekeeping, choosing to continue to wear his own decades-worn ball cap.

Willie's nurse, a twentysomething named Nicole, came into his room with a cart of food and set his lunch down next to his bed. She was dressed in mint-green scrubs and had curly, blond hair that made Willie wish he had been born fifty years later.

"Good afternoon, Willie," said Nicole, as she lifted off the plastic container covering his plate. It was Thursday, and that meant a piece of rubbery chicken, powdered mashed potatoes, a pear, and green Jell-O.

"Good afternoon," mumbled Willie as he maintained his gaze on the cemetery. He would normally greet Nicole with a smile and ask how her day was. Nicole sensed something was wrong. "I'm sorry about Leonard. I know you guys were close."

Willie replied without turning away from the window. "Yeah."

Nicole picked up his breakfast tray and placed it on the cart. "Well, I hope you enjoy your lunch." She was about to walk out of the room when Willie, under his breath, said, "It's almost like it's taunting us."

Nicole stopped and turned back to him. "What's that, Willie?"

Willie's eyes were transfixed on the swath of headstones and monuments poking out of the ground across the street. The area around Valleyview was relatively nice; there was a lush park on one side and a row of quaint, little shops on the other. But that square of granite and marble directly across the street was an ever-present reminder that his days were numbered.

He had lost seven friends to Valleyview in the past two years, and they seemed to be dying off more frequently as of late. These weren't sickly, on-their-deathbed types either; these were active seniors—bingo fanatics, swim class regulars, bridge pros. He hadn't seen so many bite the big one in such a short span of time since his days in WWII. And he knew what killed them back then—artillery, explosions, Japs. What killed these folks was a mystery.

"That damn cemetery. It sits there across the street, just waiting for us to croak. It's like some morbid assembly line— from here to there, with a funeral home somewhere in the middle. I might as well just walk on over and pour some dirt over my head. Save someone the trouble."

"Don't say that, Willie," said Nicole. She came over and rested her hand on his shoulder. "You've got a lot of *life* in you."

"That's what I thought about Leonard, but look what happened to him. He was taking us to the cleaners in backgammon one minute and then—bam! —dead as a duck."

"It just happens, Willie. There's no rhyme or reason to it. The best you can do is just keep on keepin' on."

"Right, right," said Willie. "I'll try. But don't be surprised if you find me stiff as a board tomorrow morning."

Nicole gave Willie a sympathetic smile and left the room.

Willie spent the rest of the day staring out the window, watching people come in and out of the cemetery. A fat man carrying his lunch. A couple of joggers. A rich-looking couple walking their dog. The scene outside Willie's window eventually transitioned from pleasantly sunny to stiflingly dark. He was about to lie down for the night when he saw a flash of green from across the street. He focused his eyes on it, unsure of what would be coming out of the cemetery at such an hour. His eyesight had diminished severely over the years, so making out whatever it was, especially at night, was a tall order.

It was a figure, that he knew for sure, and it was heading toward the nursing home. As it neared the door, he could finally make out what it was: a man in a mint-green outfit. Before he could get a good look at his face, however, the man walked in through the front door and out of sight.

Willie got out of bed as fast as his old bones would let him, grabbed his walker, and went out to the hallway and up to the nurses' station.

"Nicole, Nicole, I need to talk to Nicole!" shouted Willie as he approached the tall, African-American nurse behind the counter. Her name tag read 'Gladys'.

"Nicole's shift ended at 5, Mr. Morris," said Gladys. "How can I help you?"

"I saw someone...a strange-looking person, walk out of the cemetery and into this building. I couldn't get a good look at them—my eyes ain't like they used to be. Walked straight out of there like some damned ghoul, I tell ya. Who knows what they're up to!"

"Were they doing anything suspicious?"

"Well, for starters, who walks through the cemetery at this time of night? I thought they closed at dusk. I'm just worried it might be some kind of thug or Satanist or something."

Gladys rolled her eyes. "Mr. Morris. We have extra-tight security here. If any strange person tried coming in, our guards would stop them. Listen, if I see anybody suspicious, I'll let you know. What did you say this person looked like?"

"Well, he was dressed completely in green and he—" Willie stopped when he saw a man walking down the hall. He was dressed in mint-green scrubs and he was heading right toward them.

"This is Heath, Willie," said Gladys as the man neared the station. "He's worked at the Center for a couple years. They just moved him up from the first floor."

"Hi, Gladys," said Heath, smiling. He was a healthy looking, brown-haired guy with a chiseled face and a smile that could blind a man.

"Heath, this is Willie," said Gladys.

"Why, hello, Willie," said Heath. "Pleased to meet you." He stuck out his hand.

Willie reluctantly shook the man's hand. "Hmm mm. Well, I'll be going to bed now." He turned and walked away, a strange and unnerving feeling in his stomach.

On his way back to his room, Willie passed Jimmy Acel, who lived in room 344. Jimmy was sitting in his favorite vinyl chair, reading *The Big Sleep* by Raymond Chandler.

"Hi, Willie," said Jimmy.

"Hey, Jim."

Jimmy put his book down. "Shame about Leonard, huh?"

"It's a damn shame, but I can't say I'm surprised. First Ed, then Larry, now Leonard. It's like some phantom virus has hit this place. Maybe the Grim Reaper."

Jimmy puffed up his chest. "I want to see that reaper sonofabitch mess with ol' Jimmy Acel!" Jimmy was a crack pilot in WWII. Said to have shot down four German bombers in less than ten minutes in the summer of '43.

Willie cracked a smile. "He better come packing, huh?"

"You betcha!"

116

Willie said goodnight to Jimmy and returned to his bedroom. He thought briefly about the person in the cemetery again before drifting off to sleep. *Was it that Heath fella?*

The Germans were no match for Jimmy Acel back in WWII, but Death finally caught up to the soldier. The following morning, Gladys found him lying in bed, cold and blue.

Willie watched from his window as paramedics wheeled Jimmy's corpse into a Lestershire General ambulance and drove off. *Another one.*

He walked out of his room, down the hallway, and peeked into Jimmy's room. The covers on Jimmy's bed were disheveled and one of his mystery novels was still cracked open on his dresser. He looked back in the hall to see if anyone was watching, then entered the room.

He flipped through the book on the dresser and smirked at the title: *Beyond a Reasonable Death*. He had always laughed at Jimmy's pulp novels; the writing was terrible and the plots were beyond hokey.

He stopped smiling, however, when he noticed a strange symbol, written in red ink, on the title page. It was triangular, with what looked like three eyes appearing at each corner. The thing was intensely weird and gave him the willies.

He walked out of the room and down the hall, stopping by the nurses' station, where Nicole was working.

"Nicole, can you tell me who was taking care of Jimmy last night?"

Nicole looked at him with sympathy. "Willie, I'm so sorry about Jimmy—"

"Thanks, but can you tell me who was assigned to him?"

Nicole gave him an odd look and flipped through the logbook. "It was the new guy, Heath. Why do you ask?"

"Just curious."

"He's a strange guy," said Nicole. She leaned in closer and lowered her voice. "He's always smiling, but in a weird way, with this vacant look..."

Willie listened intently and nodded.

"Keep this between you and me, Willie, but he and Gladys seem a bit *too* close."

Willie perked up. "Is that right? What do you mean?"

"I've caught them talking in private. They always give me funny looks, too, like they have it out for me. Creeps me out."

Willie thought about Gladys. She had been working on the floor for only six months or so. She wasn't the warmest of nurses. She mostly kept to herself.

"Don't tell anybody what I said, Willie? This is between you and me. Okay?"

Willie nodded and returned to his room, worried for Nicole and for the rest of the folks in the building.

Later that night, Willie sat in his chair and looked out his window. The cemetery was pitch black save for the glow of a street light shining down upon the front gate. As he watched, the same strange man from the previous night emerged from the dark interior.

He sprung out of bed and went to his door. Cracking it open, he peered out into the hallway. Heath was talking to Gladys at the nurses station in hushed tones. After a minute, he left and entered the room of Judy Kirkpatrick, the floor's resident bingo all-star.

Five minutes later, Heath came out of Judy's room with a content look on his face, as if he had just finished a long and fulfilling supper.

Willie walked up to the front desk. Gladys rolled her eyes as he approached.

"Gladys, that Heath guy, where did you say he's from?"

"Why do you ask, Mr. Morris?"

Willie glared at her. "As a paying member of this establishment, I think I deserve to know who's taking care of us."

Gladys stood up and leaned toward him. "Heath is a licensed practical nurse. That's all you need to know. Now go back to your room and get some rest."

As Willie had expected, Judy was found dead the next morning. They drove her across town to Rice Funeral Home, a brief layover before they would bring her back and stick her in the ground, across the road at Valleyview.

That afternoon Willie snuck into Judy's room, looking for clues. Pictures of grandkids and relatives hung on the walls. The room smelled like mothballs and puréed meatloaf.

He picked up Judy's bingo card and flipped it around. There it was—the same triangular shape with the wicked eyes that he'd found in Jimmy's book.

Willie went back to his room, his 78-year-old heart pounding in his chest.

Despite his weak knees and bad back, Willie walked out of the nursing home that night and paid a visit to the cemetery. The nurses checked in every hour, so would have to hurry back before anyone noticed.

The graveyard felt darker than it had appeared from across the street. Headstones were completely shrouded in shadow, the names impossible to decipher by the unaided eye, in the gloom of a light ground fog.

He clicked on his flashlight and shone it on individual headstones. He didn't know what he was looking for, but he knew some answer had to lie on this plot of land. So many of his friends were buried here, and he owed it to them to find out.

GRADY. WINTERMUTE. TOM AND MARY BRILL. Names appeared in the glow of the flashlight as Willie scanned the cemetery. Twenty minutes passed. His old bones quickly tired from the strain of the nighttime search.

He stopped and gasped.

There, in the befogged light, was the symbol, almost jutting out at him from the severely weathered rock. The same emblem from Jimmy's book and Judy's bingo card. He pointed the flashlight further up the headstone and read the inscription: HEATH FARRELL. 1804 - 1844.

Willie waited in his bedroom. And waited.

When the clock struck nine, he got out of his chair and peeked out into the hallway. He watched as Heath approached the nurses station and talked to Gladys, their voices barely above a whisper.

When they finished talking, Heath went into the kitchen and came out pushing a large food cart. He went down the hallway and Willie followed, tip-toeing behind.

Heath pushed the cart into Agnes Hamilton's room and closed the door behind him.

Willie put his head against the door and listened. He heard Heath greeting Agnes and talking to her about the plants sitting on her windowsill.

The conversation ceased and Willie heard footsteps walking back toward the door. Quickly, he moved away from the door and pretended to walk down the hall. A second later, Heath came out pushing the cart. He looked at Willie, smiled, and turned the corner to the next corridor.

Willie rushed into Agnes' room, hoping there was still time to save her. But when he got inside, Agnes was wide awake watching *Wheel of Fortune*; not a scratch on her. She actually looked quite content.

"Willie Morris, what are you doing?"

"I'm sorry, Agnes. I thought I heard you call for help." He backed away and walked out of the room, feeling like a foolish, senile old man.

He took a seat next to her door and waited. He didn't know if Heath would return, and he wanted to make sure he was there if he did.

Willie woke up the next morning in the hallway, his neck aching from his awkward sleep position. He saw Agnes' room was empty, so he walked to the nurses station and greeted Gladys. "Can you tell me how Agnes Hamilton is doing?"

"Agnes? Why do you ask? Agnes is totally fine. She's down in 112, playing pinochle."

Willie felt relieved, yet utterly confused.

"Unfortunately, Violet Bradford passed away last night," continued Gladys.

Willie looked at her, dumbstruck. "Violet Bradford, down on the first floor?"

Gladys nodded.

"Who was working down there last night?"

"Nicole and I. Why do you ask?"

"No reason." He walked back to his room, unsure of what to make of the night's events. Maybe there was another Heath Farrell back in the 19th century. Maybe the name was just a coincidence and this nursing home wasn't haunted by a soul-sucking vampire.

The day passed uneventfully. Willie didn't know what to make of the death on the first floor. He went to bed early that night and was awakened by the sound of someone entering his room. He lay in bed, his eyes barely cracked open. As they slowly adjusted to the light, he could see it was Nicole. She didn't have food or medication on her, and his room didn't need to be cleaned, so he wondered what she was doing. He watched as she crept to his dresser and, strangely, picked up his Yankees cap.

An intense light suddenly formed around the cap. Willie watched in shock as Nicole slowly sucked some sort of ephemeral substance into her mouth. He shivered as her tongue lapped up the energy, a demented look in her eyes.

Willie suddenly felt a sharp pain in his chest, as if someone had jabbed him with a kitchen knife and was turning it back and forth. He felt as if his lungs were being sucked out by an industrial strength vacuum.

The door swung open and in walked Gladys. Nicole quickly dropped the hat and all of Willie's pain began to subside.

"We've got a code 5 on the first floor. Let's go," said Gladys.

Nicole and Gladys left the room and Willie got out of bed, still shaking. He walked over to the dresser and picked up the hat. Flipping it over, he saw the same strange triangular symbol burned into the brim. He didn't sleep that night.

When Nicole walked into Willie's room the next morning to drop off his breakfast, she seemed startled to see him awake.

"What's wrong, Nicole? Didn't expect to find me in such good health?" he said, smirking.

Nicole's stupefied look transformed into one of intense annoyance. "What do you *mean*, Willie?"

"Nothing. Just an old man talking nonsense. Thanks for bringing me my breakfast. Oooh, bacon and eggs."

Nicole left the room without saying another word.

Later that day, at Willie's request, Nicole accompanied him to the cemetery to visit Jimmy Acel's grave. As always, Willie wore his Yankees cap. It was evening and the sun was just beginning to approach the horizon.

"I know you weren't asleep last night," said Nicole, as they walked the gravel path.

"I'm an old man. I don't sleep that well. I have crazy dreams with all this medication you guys make me take."

"I want to show you something before we stop at Jimmy's grave. Over this way." They turned into an older, more secluded corner of the cemetery. The headstones in the section were crumbling; some of them were barely holding together.

They approached the grave. It almost felt inevitable. There, inscribed in granite, was the name: NICOLE MEYER. A small daguerreotype appeared underneath, and it looked as if it Nicole had posed for it not a week prior. Willie looked at her, aghast, and she smiled back as if she were waiting for his reaction.

"Why, Nicole?" he said gently. "Why?"

"I can't die, Willie." She grabbed his arm and he winced at the inhuman strength of this petite woman.

"I had a feeling about you, Nicole," said Gladys, who appeared from behind a mausoleum with Heath.

"We had to be sure," said Heath. "It's been so long since I've felt your presence, I'd almost forgotten your true form."

Without hesitation, Heath and Gladys rushed toward Nicole and tried to tackle her. Nicole easily dispatched Gladys, throwing her to the ground and knocking her out cold.

Heath grabbed Nicole by the arms and the two tumbled on the grass. Heath managed to get on top of her, but Nicole pushed him up and tossed him aside with ease. She stood quickly and lunged toward Willie, tackling him to the sod, wrapping her hands around his feeble head.

"Don't worry, Willie," she said. "You'll get to see Jimmy real soon."

Her lips parted and she started her sucking routine, a fantastic glow appearing around his baseball cap. But something was wrong. She started choking. Then convulsing like a cat heaving up a massive hairball. She arched her back and howled, dropping the cap and Willie to the ground.

"What? What did you do?" she said, holding the cap in her trembling hand.

The glow around the cap receded and Nicole's body began to disintegrate—her powers directed not toward Willie's energy but toward the dead aura of Jimmy Acel. The skin on her face caved inward, revealing a rotting, black skull. The rest of her body followed, her bones cracking and a vile, oozing substance draining from her, until she was reduced to a pile of putrid ash on the ground.

The trio stood silently around the remnants of Nicole. A harsh wind blew, scattering whatever remained of her throughout the cemetery. Willie picked up the cap and looked at the brim. The name "JIMMY ACEL" was written in black marker on the inside; no symbol, no curse. It had worked.

"We didn't know it was her," said Gladys, walking up to Willie with a weary look on her face.

Heath appeared behind her, and it was clear under the moonlight that he was not comprised of the same flesh and blood as Willie. He could see right through him, and could make out Jimmy's grave through his shade.

"I was her first victim."

Heath explained some of it to Willie. Some people have unfinished business and are left in between worlds with the option of improving their lot in the un-living; he had chosen to work toward a higher plane of existence. Nicole had taken the easy route, intending to occupy this world for as long as she could by draining the living of their life force.

Heath thanked Willie and Gladys before fading away into an ethereal light.

On his way home, Willie stopped by Jimmy's grave and dropped off his friend's baseball cap. He smiled as he returned to his window seat at Floral Nursing. The place across the road didn't seem quite so ominous anymore.

After the Game

Stephen trudged past the opposing team's bus in the parking lot at Greene Park. They were celebrating their late-inning win over Lestershire High when they saw him and really rubbed it in. He had made the fatal error that cost his team their freshman baseball game. The guys on the other team laughed at him and mocked his misplay as he hung his head low, bat and glove in hand for the long, lonely trek home.

He would be kicking himself over his decision for some time. He fielded the ball cleanly and threw it wide to the catcher guarding home plate instead of to first for the final out. The catcher couldn't sweep the ball down in time to tag the sliding runner and it was over. Stephen didn't bother calling his mom for a ride. It was already dusk after eleven innings of play, and he needed a long walk to cool down and sit with his disappointing performance.

Just across the street he slid into the cemetery for his usual shortcut home, leaving the busy park and taunting victors behind. It was a quiet walk, one he often took to and from the field for practice and games. He usually enjoyed the slow saunter up the long hill, through the forest and over the creek, past the high school, and finally to his house in one of the nicer neighborhoods.

Stephen dawdled in front of familiar graves. He read the names, some of whom shared his last name, some with small pictures, daguerreotypes from a different era—it distracted him for minutes at a time until his thoughts returned to baseball and his poor performance.

The sun was setting. He sat down in the grass among a less clustered patch of graves. He was a passable high school ballplayer but was getting to the age where it was clear he wasn't going to be a pro- or even college-level athlete. It was

126

easy to cry, so he did—rolling his bat in the grass, sitting next to a child's final resting place. Someone had left a plastic car from the newest Pixar movie for the kid even though the boy had been dead ten years.

He was jostled out of his self-pity and wandering thoughts by an approaching form from a little way down the hill. The caretaker had seen Stephen wander through enough. Other people jogged and walked Valleyview—maybe it was late enough where he would get a warning. He noticed he had been tapping his bat against a small, flat grave marker, probably attracting someone's attention.

Stephen didn't want to deal with an adult hassling him and stood up ready to move on. He waved off the coming form and continued up the path so as to avoid confrontation. The man was gaining on him. Stephen thought it odd that he had not been warned or greeted. He turned and continued up the gentle incline, walking backwards a short way. He saw that it was an old man in a suit, only about thirty or so yards away. By now it had become so dusky he couldn't make out much about him.

"Sorry, I'm leaving right now." Stephen hoped that was enough to get the guy to leave him alone. He turned back and quickened his pace. Not ten seconds passed when he could hear the old man gaining on him, his labored shuffling. He was surprised the man could keep up.

"Sir, I had a late game. I'll be out of here in a couple minutes." He didn't bother turning for a response and kept pumping his feet. He was getting worried that this old fellow might not be with the cemetery, but someone who had followed him in. Stephen considered the possibility that his trailer was some sort of molester or abductor—but the thought didn't stick when he remembered he was a solid six feet and could really swing a bat.

The man in the suit was now on his heels. He was getting back some of that adrenaline that had seeped out of him after the final play of the ball game and was ready to run. The man groaned behind him and Stephen practically jumped out of his cleats. He spun to confront the man.

"Gimme a break, dude—what's up?" The guy didn't respond and had a wild look on his face which genuinely frightened the teen. He lunged at Stephen, grabbing his jersey. Stephen yelled and jumped back, releasing himself. He pushed the guy back with the edge of the bat then ran off the path and into a maze of large headstones and mausoleums.

Unfortunately, running through a cemetery near dark isn't the safest of options, and he soon tripped over a small, flat grave marker and twisted his ankle enough to yelp in torment. He grabbed his glove and bat and jumped up to feel a sharp, shooting pain radiating from his ankle through his leg, and fell back down to the ground with a loud groan.

"Ah, shit...," Stephen sighed in a near whisper, clutching his hurt leg. He could hear the old man in the suit groaning and shuffling in his direction, so he crawled between two nearby mausoleums and hoped the creepy guy had dementia and would forget he was chasing him.

He hid in his cubbyhole, collecting himself for a few minutes, before the man appeared and again lunged at him, grabbing at his jersey and knocking the cap off his head. He prodded and jabbed the man back, afraid to actually hurt the old guy, who was obviously not all there.

"C'mon man, leave me the hell alone! Don't make me actually hit you with this bat!" Stephen thought of his own grandpa at Floral Nursing and Rehabilitation Center. He didn't even remember his own wife due to his advanced Alzheimer's. This senile guy pawing at him was probably somebody's grandpa. The out-of-control man in the suit eventually backed off from some of the harder jabs to the chest.

Stephen was breathing heavy, waiting to hear the shuffling again. When five minutes passed, he got up on his now swollen ankle and used the bat as a crutch to begin limping out into the open.

"Goddammit!" The crazy old coot tackled him and tore at his jersey and pants, tossing the bat in his melee against the young man. Stephen screamed in abject fear of being a six-foot-something, fifteen-year-old cemetery rape victim, abused by a groaning, wheezing octogenarian.

Thwack! The elderly man's head cleaved a foot above Stephen. Some blood spurted onto his cheek and neck as the man in the suit shuddered then crumpled on top of the teen. Stephen recognized the axe man instantly.

"Jesus! What the hell is going on?!" He practically screamed at the caretaker, shocked that he had just axed an old man in the head. The middle-aged, grizzled cemetery employee wiped his axe and reached down to help Stephen to his feet.

"Get up, kid. Let's go call your parents." Stephen stood with some effort and was supported by the caretaker as he hobbled back down the hill toward the service shack.

Stephen called his mom to come get him. He said he had fallen in the cemetery and sprained his ankle.

"I can't believe you axed that old man in the head!" The older man just looked at him funny and smirked.

"Sorry, kid, I lost track of the guy. I usually get them in the ground before they start walking. There were a bunch of kids here earlier trying to desecrate Schwartz's Tomb. Had a hell of a time rounding 'em up and kicking 'em out." Stephen just looked at him dumbfounded. "Four feet of dirt and sod is usually enough to keep them down. I got distracted after his funeral and left him hanging, and... you know."

"You're telling me that guy was dead?!" The caretaker nodded. Stephen was in a state of disbelief. Everything after he left the ball field now seemed to take on an otherworldly quality.

"Looks like your mom's here." A car pulled up in front of the small shack. Stephen stood with his bat and glove to leave, but paused in the doorway to thank the man.

"Well, I'm glad you helped me out back there, whether that guy was living or dead...so, thanks."

"No problem. I should've gotten to him sooner and none of this would've happened. For whatever reason, it seems to be more of a common occurrence these days." The caretaker smiled and waved Stephen off, then stopped him as if he forgot to add something. "And kid, let's keep this between you and me." The caretaker winked at him and he nodded an affirmative before slipping out the door and into his mom's car.

Pact and Principle

Jonathan nervously waited at the child's grave for the parents to arrive. He was never sure how it would go, but it was an easy buck, and in some twisted way he thought maybe he was helping people find closure.

The couple soon arrived, recognizing Jonathan from his website. "You must be the medium?" asked the man. Jonathan shook his hand; the wife was still distraught and distant, due to her recent loss.

"Yes, sir. Mr. and Mrs. King?" They nodded. He continued, "I've been honing in on your son for most of the afternoon. I think I have a clear channel to receive any message he may have." He lied.

"Can he talk?" The woman spoke, her lip quivering. The psychic felt a momentary pang of guilt but continued the reading.

"Yes, I think so. Gary's worried about his pet...dog, er, cat." He searched the parents' faces; he was going to have to do this cold. He kicked himself for not at least looking up their Facebook profiles.

"*What* about him?" The father's pleasant affect diminished into a slight scowl. Jonathan was starting to sweat.

"He says he's worried the cat will miss him."

The woman shook her head and walked off.

"Gary hated that cat. You should be ashamed of yourself." The father shook off Jonathan's further attempts at salvaging the session and the medium watched his two hundred dollars walk off.

Jonathan paced the cemetery, irritated that he had wasted his time and jeopardized his relatively good brand due to a no-show. Various spirits tried to gain his attention, but he ignored them.

"The boy should be here; it's seven days since. Why isn't he here?" He stormed through a number of apparitions, clear as day to him but no one else living. Many begged him to assist them in some way, some with a specific purpose, others merely caught up in the trappings of the living.

"What? You want me to help you?" He admonished a particularly persistent and ghastly woman, "You died in 1920. Anyone who cared about you is long dead." She vanished and he could still hear her ethereal sobbing as he made his way toward a newer section of the cemetery.

"Is there anyone present who has left the world of the living this century?" *It's getting harder to make a living out here.* "No one? That's what I thought." He started up the hill toward that day's burial. He knew it would be a long shot trying to contact one of the freshly departed. It took a few days for spirits to find their land legs—but he was getting desperate for business.

As Jonathan ascended the hill he saw a dark figure under the tent at the new burial site. He assumed it was a priest and hesitated, as most priests and theologians knew him well and hated him because he could provide services well beyond their abilities. It was better that Jonathan hadn't continued up that path, as his day went from very bad to horrendous when the figure rose over the open coffin and separated the spirit from the corpse.

Oh, boy. The medium spun on a dime and hoped he hadn't been spotted. He fully intended to leave Valleyview and never return, but he was stopped by an older, familiar, and unusually corporeal apparition with surprising strength.

"Give me a break. I can't help you," Jonathan said.

The former caretaker, Charlie, held him tight. "You know what's going on back there, Jon. How are you going to just walk out?" The medium shook his suit jacket off into the ghost's hands and continued toward the exit.

"Watch me." Jonathan jogged out of the cemetery and went home.

Two weeks passed and Jonathan needed to get back to business. He tried out some of the newer cemeteries, but they were proverbial ghost towns compared to Valleyview. He had debated going back for days, but ultimately that was where the money was. So he returned to try and conjure up some fresh spirits.

A number of ghosts lined the fence, pleading their cases as he walked to the main entrance. "Sir, my daughter...You've got to tell my daughter not to turn on the range. I'm afraid there's been a terrible gas leak." The messages seemed to all run together, merging in a mishmash of tragedy.

"My husband killed my father."

"Daddy, is that you?"

"They drowned the lot of them in the river."

Jonathan had heard their stories countless times. He was on the lookout for someone new who was ready to communicate. He could always sense more spirits, but it took time for some to reveal themselves.

As he walked the paths through the cemetery, he noticed that the other side had become eerily quiet—then he saw the shadow. Even the dead were hiding from *it*. The demon was perched on a mausoleum, waiting for something, possibly waiting for him—but he wasn't going to hang around and find out.

Jonathan made a beeline for the exit, sure whatever it was had seen him and was watching him. Charlie appeared and easily kept pace with the psychic.

"There are plenty of innocent folks in here, Jon. You're just going to up and walk out on them?"

"You of all people...er, former people, should talk, Charlie." The ghost was surprised he knew his name.

"I'm making my amends, Jon." Charlie had taken it upon himself to be a shepherd of sorts—Valleyview's own concierge to the dead.

"This has nothing to do with me, pal."

"He's been here for months now, Jon. From what I hear, this is the only game in town. What are you gonna do when this demon's collected every lost soul before you can wring your dollar out?" The apparition had a point.

Jonathan stopped just outside the main gate to consult the old spirit through the cemetery fence. "I'm not a demonologist, or an exorcist for that matter. I channel the dead for a living. I make my money; everyone gets what they want."

Charlie shook his head at the narrow-minded psychic. "I'm afraid an exorcist wouldn't help much in this case. This *thing* is of the elemental variety, and has been coming and going for a couple centuries now." Charlie had been one of many complicit caretakers who looked the other way when the demon was fed by the cemetery owners.

"This isn't 1955. The Valleyview LLC isn't owned by the Lesters anymore—and I really should be going. I don't want to become acquainted with that creature." Jonathan knew much of the local history, having lived his whole life in Lestershire.

The ghost shook his head at the sometimes conman. "Give me another minute, son. There may be a board of directors now, but I assure you, the pact has passed on."

"What pact? ...Wait, I get what you're saying. You're going to tell me Lester made a deal with the devil and that's how the family gained their fortune." The ghost grabbed Jonathan by his tie through the iron fence and yanked him so they were face to face, the dead man revealing his true, tormented visage. Jon shuddered and tried to pull back.

"You think this demon is messin' around up there?"

Jon shook his head. Charlie released him and returned to a more pleasant affect before continuing, "But in a matter of speaking, yes. The great Harry Lester parlayed a land deal that his great-grandfather made into a wealthy factory town."

Jon sighed. "I'm assuming it's more complicated than that?"

Charlie knew that this particular shyster medium was the only one who could help. He had never come across a living soul with quite the reach into the world of the dead as Jonathan.

"When General Clinton cleared this land of natives and drove them from the banks of the Quee-Hanna River, Charles Lester made a deal with a local Indian tribe. They leased him their land in return for supplies and aid in escaping, with the understanding that someday they would return. Lester was a pioneer out here and had an established trading post for twenty years before the expansion west. This was great farming land. Generations of Lesters grew the family business leasing land to Dutch immigrants and amassing the wealth that Harry eventually used to build the first factory. However, the Indians left something behind as a guarantee that their contract with Lester was binding."

Jonathan interjected, "They left a demon behind...to do what exactly?"

"Their shaman, the land and the demon are all one and the same. He's bound to the land and he's determined to fulfill the pact Lester made with his tribe. This *thing*'s been growing more powerful each generation, taking souls and lives as payment, even reaching beyond the cemetery."

"I'm not following. How have the Lesters been able to benefit from having a murderous elemental on their land?"

"The demon only became a nuisance to Harry Lester when he filled this land with people, houses, and factories. When the creature appeared on the hillside one evening, he panicked and tried to pay the debt all at once. The factory fire in aught-five was one of his attempts to feed the beast. It didn't quite work out as he had planned, and his son, Donald, was the one who built this cemetery and figured out how to undermine the reach of the demon."

Jonathan again interjected, "By feeding it the souls of the dead after burial?"

"More or less. My father was the caretaker before me. He determined that it only needed a few souls each year to be satiated, and that it had no power in the new portion of the cemetery across the road. So we would bury the bodies outside the creature's domain and it wouldn't reappear for years, until there was some sort of accidental death within or very near the cemetery.

"The beast was confined to cemetery grounds and enough folk were dying to feed him, but he's since grown hungrier and powerful enough to draw people in. He's taking the innocent, elderly, even children. So the ownership has from time to time buried new bodies in the old cemetery, and even resorted to select living sacrifices, I'm afraid. It won't be long now until the demon can venture out into the valley and take lives and souls as he pleases."

Jonathan was horrified. Had he known any of this he would have left town years ago. Elementals, demons, and shadow forms hated the living, especially the few that could sense them.

"I can't deal with this. That thing will kill me if it knows I'm around. I've already stayed too long. Best of luck against that thing."

Jonathan walked the sidewalk, spirits trailing him on the other side of the fence, begging him not to leave just yet. He looked back one last time before he turned the corner. Charlie shook his head at him and vanished.

*　　*　　*

Jonathan was visited in a dream by a young boy who had recently passed. The boy was desperate to contact his parents and provide them comfort in their grieving. Since the boy had recently been buried in Valleyview, Jonathan would have to risk being found out by the demon if he wanted the payday.

He chose the easy money, and returned to the cemetery he vowed to never again step foot in (for as long as it had a soul-sucking, murderous inhabitant, anyway.) Charlie was nowhere to be found, for once, and Jonathan soon located the spirit of the boy.

"Will your parents come? What will you tell them when they arrive?" Jon went through his usual series of questions when meeting a new candidate, as if he was interviewing them for a job.

"My mom is on the edge and my Dad is distant and doesn't know that she might hurt herself. You have to get them to come here together so nothing bad happens."

Jon attempted to comfort the spirit and assured him he would make the connection for him.

The boy faded and Jon made his way back toward the exit. He wondered where Charlie was, and figured the former caretaker would have another earful for him. He stopped in front of a familiar grave and the crying woman appeared.

"Ma'am, have you seen that old caretaker, Charlie?"

She nodded and spoke, "His grandson is supposed to be buried today. He is with family."

Jonathan felt an odd impulse to see Charlie and offer him his condolences. He walked the path up the old cemetery hill to what appeared to be a family plot. As he crested he saw Charlie being forcefully handled, his aura fading as the demon drew away his energy. This was all within view of what Jonathan assumed was Charlie's grandson's casket. He hid behind a stone and watched the beast dominate and control the old ghost.

Jonathan felt panicked and disturbed, but couldn't imagine how he could aid in any way. It was pretty clear that Charlie was trying to prevent the demon from stealing his grandson's spirit, certainly a losing battle for any solitary ghost.

That was when it hit him. There was a cemetery of a countless number around him. Surely, their combined force could overwhelm one solitary, elemental, he thought. He whispered, "I know you're present. I can practically feel a dozen of you breathing down my neck back here... How many of you have I connected with your loved ones over the years?" No response from the gallery he was sure was witnessing the end of Charlie as an entity.

"How many of you has Charlie helped during your stay here? I've seen for quite some time how he's guided and cared for the newly disembodied. Think about how disoriented you were for those first few hours, days, and weeks. Who helped you accept your current situation?" No specter rose to the occasion.

Jonathan swallowed his fear and made a rash decision. He ran toward the unfolding scene with the demon—and as he dashed wildly into the fray, his terror subdued by an unnamable fount of selfless inspiration.

The charge itself was startling enough that the demon actually turned his attention from Charlie and released him. The creature postured and expanded into its full eight-foot frame, towering over Jonathan. Its emaciated, clawed hand emerged from under its heavy robe and found a home in Jonathan's chest—stopping him mid-run and ending his life almost instantly.

Blood poured from Jonathan's mouth as the demon removed its hand and turned back to Charlie and the casket which held his grandson. Charlie maintained his flickering, partial form with the last of his energy. He did not have enough power to remain fully-bodied and could not manage to re-enter the second plane of existence without dissipating into the ether.

Charlie was about to be finished by the elemental, and to witness his grandson's soul consumed, when a silent army formed around the demon. Many of the spirits, having taken Jonathan's words to heart, and after seeing his lone charge against the demon, were emboldened to join the confrontation.

They overwhelmed the heinous beast. Many were destroyed, vanished from any kind of earthly existence during the violent struggle. Those that remained forced the elemental back into the earth from where it came. A great deal of the creature's power was lost when they destroyed its terrestrial form.

Jonathan was not long dead before he was led back to the cemetery by the former caretaker. For some time, he and Charlie worked together to guide and acclimate new souls there at Valleyview. Eventually, due to his selfless sacrifice, Jonathan was allowed to pass into an existence and plane beyond the reach of elementals, demons, worldly worry, and strife.

Appendix A: *A Secret History of Lester Shoe and Boot, 1905-1910*, by Anonymous

Foreman Frick would pace the roof of the tannery building at Lester Boot Co., always with a thick cigar in hand. He did not particularly like cigars, but was fond of the authority a nice fat stogie seemed to impart. He had an endless supply since his boss, Harry Lester, had purchased the local cigar rolling factory the previous year. Frick would have preferred to be running the cigar rollers as opposed to the stinking vats and lime pits of the tannery, but he made do and, by all accounts, ran an efficient factory.

The morning of August 16th was like most mornings. Frick walked his path, thinking of his future while his charges toiled away in the sweltering factory below. Lester had promised him a plot of land up near the hill on the north side of the village. Soon he would be able to build his own house for his wife and young boy within sight of Lester's mansion. He was not quite Harry Lester's right-hand man but knew it was only a matter of time.

At the time, Frick was running the most profitable component of Lester's boot business. He produced leather from local cattle at an astounding rate. His workers were paid by the piece of hide processed and not by the hour like the boot workers in the other factories, and he made sure his quota was met each and every day.

Summer was the worst on the workers, the window slats opened a little more than twelve inches. Frick's motivation for his workers was the sweltering heat, and in winter the unruly cold could still be counted on for an accelerated rate of production. He would often lock the doors to the shops and would not let them have their lunch until the morning's quota was met.

Lester let Frick sell surplus processed leather to the furniture makers and pocket a dollar per hide. On the morning of the 16th his calculation and tabulation of future profits was interrupted by the acrid smell of burning lye and smoking animal fat. Frick bounded down the stairs from the roof, his portly belly bouncing as he stumbled along each flight. While he slowly made his way from the rooftop, the tannery workers choked on smoke and scrambled for the windows and smashed against the three doors.

The fire had grown monstrous, fed by all the chemical accelerants that the tannery used for hair and fat removal during the leather-making process. Some men were able to squeeze out of the thin slats of the windows, others futilely smashed with their wood and metal tools at the iron-enforced windowpanes.

Not every man panicked on the factory floor that day. A Lithuanian-born immigrant, who had been a fire brigadier, quickly covered his face with a wet cloth and went down to the lower pits to lead men to the ladders so that they would have a fighting chance. Two Slovaks joined him and pulled countless gagging, choking men to the windows, which three Polish brothers had managed to pry open wide enough that even the burliest of men could squeeze through. How the trio managed to get those windows open remains a mystery.

As the last of the men trickled out through the smoking windows, nearly a hundred of their compatriots puked and wheezed on the ground nearby. When Frick scurried to the front door and unlocked it, just inside lay six bodies crumpled on the floor—the smoke so thick and unbearable that the six had no hope of finding their way back to the exit they had made. A few of the men risked further injury by retrieving the dead.

There was nearly a riot outside the factory when it was clear Frick had not called the fire brigade. He nervously stood behind a row of armed Pinkertons while he shouted orders to the medics and hospital staff that had arrived to treat the infirm.

*   *   *

"Frank, you did what you could." Frick met with Harry Lester in his office; both had cigars in hand. Lester fully enjoyed everything about smoking and practically wallowed from sun-up to sundown in smoke.

"Thank you, Mr. Lester." The pair shared a knowing smile.

"I'd like to give you the cigar factory, but I need you to do me a favor," said Lester. Frick was surprised and a little disappointed, as he had done everything Lester had ever asked of him.

"Of course, Mr. Lester..." said Frick. Lester had promised him land two years previous on the condition that Frick produce better numbers than his predecessor. Frick momentarily wondered if he would ever see that land.

"Frank, the six that died—they have no one to claim them. Will you make sure they're buried and it's kept quiet?" Frick momentarily wavered in his dedication.

"Sir, where exactly should they be buried?" The immigrant and pauper cemetery had been past capacity since the cholera outbreak of 1903. Lester mulled it over.

"That plot of land between the Valleyview Golf Course and the new company store." Neither of which had been built but were plotted on the map on Lester's wall, as it included both his current and future developments. It was one of the last few open spaces among Lester's holdings and the location Frick had imagined for his future home.

"Sir, we talked a few years back about land for a house..."

Lester smirked at his employee. "Yes, yes—I haven't forgotten. Bury the dead and build your family a nice home, Frick."

"On the burial?" Lester nodded and hunched over to light a new cigar. Frick turned to go perform his task when Lester stopped him.

"And Francis, bring along men you trust. You know..." Frick agreed and left.

The following evening an intoxicated Frick lead his little band to his future land holding with a large freight cart pulled by a team of horses. They removed the six shrouded corpses and began digging, by hand, six graves under lantern light. Soon his little group began complaining of the workload and the added difficulty of a particularly muggy August night.

"Mr. Frick, we've made very little headway—we'll be here all night." Intoxicated, Frick could care less about his workers but he certainly did not want to be out all night getting eaten by mosquitos.

"Dig one hole then, a concentrated effort." Frick burped and sat back on the wagon. Two of the men protested, but were quickly quieted by their fellows.

Hours deep into the night the men unceremoniously tossed the six brave men into the cold dank hole in the ground, one on top of the other. A heavy fog rolled in covering the grave. Frick was fast asleep in his own bed before three that morning.

*　　*　　*

It was a year before Frick would begin building his house. He had forgotten precisely where he had buried those men as he was inebriated at the time. The tannery was not rebuilt, instead Lester quickly began importing shoe leather ready to press into boots, leading to the loss of hundreds of jobs. So,

144

without a tannery to run, Frick was given free rein of the cigar factory—which itself was struggling due to a Caribbean influx of cheap tobacco product.

The Lester employees held a grudge toward Francis Frick that only intensified the years he spent unsuccessfully attempting to resurrect the North American cigar business. Rumor spread of possible insurance fraud as Lester had gotten a windfall at his factory's demise and there was only one candidate tying the death of those six workers to Harry Lester's questionable business practices.

When Frick returned to the boot factory as foreman things were very different. The workers did not respond as they did in the old days. Tools and machines were damaged, product was flawed. Frick blamed it on the unions, the guys in the boot shop whispered that it was ghosts from the past. Productivity fell until he was demoted by the new owner, Lester's son and heir, Donald.

Francis Frick lived for less than four years in his new home, which came to lie between the company store and the new community cemetery. Donald Lester was not as untouchable as his father and usually made concessions when his workers made noise. A free cemetery was built for the employees and their families as opposed to a golf course and country club as his father had imagined.

Frick was miserable his final years. He could not walk the streets at night out of fear of old reprisal and was constantly harassed when the first telephones were wired. His son would tell the tale long after all the factories were shuttered, how his father was unable to sleep at night—how he would mutter about all the nasty voices over the telephone. In 1910, Mrs. Frick found her husband hanging in the basement of his long dreamt of home.

Appendix B: *The Black Book*

The following is a brief excerpt from the Indian translation found among Jerome Javitz's possessions. His car was found partly submerged in the Quee-hanna River in the summer of '74. Most of his books and papers were water damaged. His body was not recovered, and he is assumed to have drowned in the river.

A shaman is capable of casting sickness spells on the body. Their power comes from charms—from skins, stones, herbs, animal bones—but more power can be conjured from human bones.

The crow is a vessel which the shaman may use to separate himself from the living world and enter the realm of ancestors and demons. The crow is the spiritual guide between worlds. From the possessed realm a shaman may gain possession and control over other entities and disrupt the path of the natural order.

A shaman only has power directed and absorbed from certain land. The shamanic spirit is bound to land for an indefinite period. Once in possession of a new vessel, the shaman may leave his land for periods of time to do his work but may not venture far from tribal territory.

Burial places, old and new, sacred and accidental, are most often the grounds from which a shaman operates. He will take on the form of a demon or a child or an animal and gather spirits to him to empower his pursuits, private grudges, and tribal feuds.

To break these spells a medicine man should induce vomiting, sing the songs of the incarnate demon spirit, and fire weapons to scare them. The possessed should be submerged in a stream or river until drowning. If disrupted correctly, the demon should be exorcised and the original spirit should return to the vessel.

To separate a shaman from the land where he draws his power is not possible. The goal of the medicine man is to keep his enemy confined to a small area so he cannot pollute his surroundings and impinge on the lives of the living tribe.

Appendix C: *A Cemetery Garland,*
by Eric Verlaine

(Friendship)

We counted the stones
and slabs,
from here to the end
and back;
the percentage
of flowered beds,
from fresh to wilty
to inorganic

(Ardor)

That so Night's shadow not fall, unappeased,
I walk with you among the trees,
for when we wend our way back home,
and I find myself by way your cemetery,
I may recall a love felt beneath the sheet,
while you lie, altogether, fast asleep

(Betrayal)

He pinned his cemetery letters
to the sweater in your shadow,
where each note had rung true,
'til the night you came to him
much too warm to the touch;
and it was evident that some body
had kept you occupied that morning

(Separation)

Lazy bones sat in her mausoleum
waiting for her boy to come
and take her to the dance,
never taking it upon herself
to find her own way from the curb,
maybe to the curb and back,
but never all the way to the dance.

Who would he dance with
if he went without her?
-she often wondered

(Resurrection)

I said I'd find my way back to you
by the cemeteries,
I remember the drive to your home
with no maps to speak of,
the soul of each cemetery
in ordered rows to guide;

I found our picnic blanket
in the churchyard,
we'd left it in the rain
under an elmy obelisk
for your home to take me back home,
and if the church is abandoned
we can make it our own

NOTES

Angel Music:

Schicksalslied is the name of a choral work by Johannes Brahms. It is based on a poem by German poet Friedrich Hölderlin. *Schicksalslied* is most often translated as "Song of Destiny."

Married, Buried:

The title of this story is taken from a chorus lyric in Nirvana's "All Apologies," which appeared on the rock band's album *In Utero*.

This story, in which adulterous characters pay the ultimate price for their infidelity, was inspired by the suspense thrillers of Alfred Hitchcock.

Other Voices, Other Tombs:

The title of this story is a play on Truman Capote's *Other Voices, Other Rooms*, a novel about children growing up in the American South listening in on conversations beyond their narrow worldview.

"Bin gar keine Russin, stamm' aus Litauen, echt deutsch." is the twelfth line of T.S. Eliot's *The Waste Land*. It comes from the section entitled, "Burial of the Dead" and is loosely translated as, "I'm not Russian at all, I come from Lithuania, pure German."

The "We three brothers" motif is inspired by an Onondaga Reservation translation of the song of the "Younger Brothers."

The setting and 'history' is distinctly Leatherstocking Country of Upstate New York. The Lester Brothers Boot and Shoe Company was the precursor to the Endicott Johnson Corporation. Little is known about the Lester Brothers operation before it was sold.

Cigar rolling was big business in the area before shoemaking. The authors' hometown, Johnson City, was founded between the Lester Brothers selling their company to a man named Endicott, and the transition from cigar rolling to shoemaking. The new owners would go on to grow the company into the world's largest shoe manufacturer and a magnet for thousands of immigrants looking to make a living in America.

The Caretaker:

Drowning Memories was the name of a punk rock band that the authors knew in high school.

The scene in which Zeke turns to wave goodbye to the caretaker, who has suddenly disappeared, is loosely inspired by the legend of The Vanishing Hitchhiker.

A Matter of Course:

This short tale is reminiscent of the interactive stories associated with the "Black Aggie" statue in Maryland and the "Black Agnus" cemetery statue in Vermont. Often some nonbeliever is challenged to spend the night in the presence of the statues to test whether or not they animate.

All Hallow's Eve:

It's common legend that on October 31st the dead are able to mingle with the living.

Knocking Back:

The authors have taken trips to test out legends over the years. The mausoleum with the green door that one knocks on (expecting the ghost to knock back) is quickly becoming one of the most well-known ghost stories in Central New York. If you're traveling on Route 8 toward West Edmeston and see a mausoleum set into a hillside (not far from the road) why not stop and see if Eunice knocks back?

Out to Lunch:

This tale was inspired by the many legends telling of people finding, stealing, and borrowing items from a cemetery which ultimately leads to their demise. Instead of removing the victim from the cemetery and having trouble follow them home, the victim, in this case a glutton, embraces the cemetery as his place of comfort while he fuels his vice.

Scry the Crow:

This atypical story was inspired by TV shows from the late 1980s and early 1990s, such as *Unsolved Mysteries*, where disappearances, legends, and murders were presented as news stories for entertainment purposes. Many of these stories would project multiple answers to mysteries and reasons for horrible crimes, including Satanism, devil worship, witchcraft, and human sacrifice. This type of storytelling entered the mainstream news from time to time, and the culture accepted the existence of avowed worshipers of the Christian Devil without scrutiny.

The native shaman as powerful wizard isn't a strong mid-Atlantic or New England Ameri-Indian archetype. The traditional shaman in American storytelling can be found in such works as *The Exorcist* and *Rosemary's Baby*, where the powerful wizard working in the realm of magic is a Catholic priest or a coven of witches devoted to the Christian Satan and his resurrection.

The tomb with the window is another old tale in Central New York. A young boy told his father he didn't want to die because he was afraid of the dark, so the man built him a tomb with a window. The authors have visited the grave, near Oxford, NY. In the 1970s, it is said that a "devil worshiper," and son of a judge, broke into the boy's tomb and stole the skull, using it for nefarious rituals.

Vermin:

This story features several nods to Stephen King's *Cujo* and Alfred Hitchcock's *The Birds*.

Dead Can Dance:

The story is named after an English-Australian music group popular in the 1980s.

Eric's fascination with the dead in the cemetery, who had "loves and hates and passions just like him," was inspired by the song "Cemetry Gates" by the English rock band The Smiths.

With overtly evil bullies, alcohol-fueled parties, and references to New Wave bands, the story bears many similarities to 80s teen movies, in particular *The Karate Kid*.

Easy Prey:

The Vanishing Hitchhiker is a motif that tells of a repetitive haunting where a woman waits for a man to pick her up and give her a ride home. He's often found entertaining her at a community dance. In this version, the vanishing ghost was married and protective of her living husband. There are versions of the story that reward the person who aids the ghost, and far older fairy tales, such as the young prince who neglects, or even harms, a beggar, only to discover it was a test that he has failed.

Randall's Complex:

The swamp-like creature that stalks Randall was meant to bear a resemblance to a malevolent creature that appears in the *Star Trek: The Next Generation* episode "Skin of Evil."

Moira's Homecoming:

The idea of human sacrifice to enrich the land, or return a special quality to the land, can be found throughout Sir James George Frazer's *The Golden Bough*, specifically the chapter entitled "Human Sacrifices for the Crops." It wasn't enough that Richie helped birth a future leader of the cult; he had to be planted in the cursed land as part of its restoration. The witchcraft and ultimate betrayal in this tale is inspired by David Pinner's *Ritual* and the subsequent British and American films entitled *The Wicker Man*.

One Foot in the Grave:

The Big Sleep is a hard-boiled crime novel by Raymond Chandler. The title is a slang term for death.

The idea of putting a hex on an object to drain life energy from the owner is featured in numerous voodoo and witchcraft stories.

After the Game:

The twist in this zombie tale is inspired by James Rolfe's short film *The Deader the Better* where the caretaker's main task is to kill a graveyard full of newly risen zombies each night. In "After the Game" the ballplayer's run-in with the shambling old man is anything but routine. Americans are asking themselves more and more what they can, or should do, when faced with violent mental illness.

Pact and Principle:

In the late 1990s and early 2000s, a number of TV mediums were popular with the general public. Audiences in studios, live in gymnasiums and school auditoriums entertained the notion that these psychics could connect them with their deceased loved ones. This was a very lucrative business for a time. Over the past ten to fifteen years, these spiritualists have faded from the mainstream culture, likely due to the success of skeptics in revealing the deceitful tactics of the mediums.

The generals mentioned, Sullivan and Clinton, swept the remaining loyalists and their native counterparts from the frontier (Western New York) of the nation during the Revolutionary War. The story imagines that a certain loyalist made a deal with a native tribe, on the banks of the river, for their land in exchange for aiding their escape from the murderous Sullivan-Clinton Expedition.

ACKNOWLEDGMENTS

Thanks to Burt, Bryan, Kiera, Pete K., Pete D., Jim, and Jasper's Minions for reading these stories and providing us with valuable feedback. Special thanks to our wives and wonderful children.

Made in the USA
Columbia, SC
10 November 2017